THE ROAD FROM ODESSA

The Odessa Trilogy

THOMAS L. GOODMAN

Praise for

The Road From Odessa

A well-written multigenerational tale spanning the globe from Odessa, Ukraine to Boston, Miami, Upstate New York and Havana. Goodman's development of characters is deep, as they navigate their complex cultural and economic environment. A must read. **Richard Hale, author of The Lunch.**

Goodman gives us a gripping story that pulsates with the struggle of an unforgettable period in history. It follows complex characters forced to face unimaginable choices. With riveting twists and turns, it is a compelling read. **Debra Edmans, author of Pointe Us Forward.**

Rum runners and rabbis, gangsters and classical musicians, The Road from Odessa is a riveting novel of one family over generations whose story begins in Odessa, Russia and ends during World War II in the United States. It is a novel full of suspense and intrigue in which the reader will be treated in gritty detail to a little told history of the dark underside of the American Jewish immigrant experience. The Stein family, at the center of the novel, rises to fame and riches only to see their fortunes turn at the hands of assassins and unpredictable, tragic events. This is a story of chutzpah, not to be missed. **Steven P. Schneider, Professor of Creative Writing, University of Texas Rio Grande Valley, author of Borderlines: Drawing Border Lives.**

Goodman is a gifted writer with the ability to weave complex fictional characters into historical settings. The Road from Odessa keeps you on the edge of your seat, as each chapter unfolds. It is a book you simply can't put down once you start it. **Constance Clarke, author of Clarke Fables.**

In his second novel, Goodman reveals himself to be a true storyteller. In this fast-paced, smart-read set during the transformational era of the 20th century, he takes us on a wild ride through the most influential cities of the day as we are introduced to some of the most recognizable figures in the world of early jazz. Set amidst the brutal world of criminal enterprise, he brings to life the struggles of one man and his determination, resilience, and willingness to do whatever it takes to survive. Buckle up! **Nancy Gort, author of 12 children's books, Professional Pianist, and Illustrator.**

I just finished reading your new novel. Wow! It was so fast-paced, and the characters were so well developed. I felt like I really knew all the generations of the family. I think with the way you ended, there will be a sequel. **Gail Salk, Reading Specialist, Upstate New York.**

The Road from Odessa is a thriller of a story starting in the 19th-century Russian Empire, where the ancestors of the protagonist were forced into a life of crime in order to support their families during periods of antisemitism and pogroms. The author colorfully describes both life in the "Old World" and the challenges faced by many new Americans as they transitioned into the "Promised Land". History buffs will especially enjoy Tom Goodman's rich historical settings. **Dr. James Strosberg, author of Two Years on the Cheyenne River Sioux Tribe Reservation.**

The Road from Odessa is firmly planted in history, beginning at the turn of the century, entwined with stories of the Schteinkov family. The twists and turns of the family story proceed sometimes in a leisurely manner, sometimes fast-paced and horrifying, especially toward the end of the novel. Goodman's weaving of family, Russian and world history, both the horror and the insidiousness of antisemitism as well as the conflicted and criminal mind, shows an active imagination that captures the reader's deepest emotions. **Elizabeth Dunn, Psychiatric Social Worker, Upstate New York.**

Once again, Goodman has spun an engaging tale, chock full of compelling characters, rich in historical detail and moral complexity. **James Salk, Town Justice, Ithaca, New York.**

Compelling and entertaining, The Road from Odessa keeps the reader engaged and the action moving. Goodman weaves the complicated lives of the story's protagonists with colorful underworld characters in exciting cultural and political times. His concise and descriptive language places the reader in the center of the action and leaves the reader wanting more. **Joan Brooks**, **Business Woman, former Private School Administrator.**

Also written by Thomas L Goodman

The Bookie's Daughter

The Road From Odessa

Editor: Mark Mathes

Paperback design/formatting: Nancy Gort

Ebook design: Nancy Koucky

Cover art: Stephanie Lambert

By Thomas L. Goodman

Published by T. L. Goodman Press

ISBN 979-8-9948772-2-7 (paperback)
ISBN 979-8-9948772-3-4 (e-book)

10 9 8 7 6 5 4 3 2

To my wife, Cynthia, and my three daughters, Alyssa, Alexandra, and Molly, with love, respect, and admiration

CONTENTS

PART III

PART IV

ACKNOWLEDGEMENTS

Thank you first to my best friends, my wife, Cynthia, and my three daughters, Alyssa, Alexandra, and Molly, for their love, support, and encouragement.

Mark Mathes, my intelligent and experienced editor, has been nothing short of kind, patient, positive, honest, straightforward and flexible. His guidance has been invaluable.

Dick Hale has been in my corner since day one, always available for writing, organizing, and plain old living suggestions.

Joan Brooks and Elizabeth Dunn are always there to make helpful suggestions in my quest to be a better writer.

Stephanie Lambert catches the true feeling of The Road from Odessa with her warm artistic talent.

Nancy Gort has been hardworking and devoted to creating the cover design, formatting and look that I was hoping for.

THOMAS L. GOODMAN

BOOK II

of

The Odessa Trilogy

THE ROAD FROM ODESSA

PART I

Chapter 1
The Fox

"They called him the Fox," said Nikolai to his eight-year-old son Moishie as they sat together in the moonlight. Their backs to the trunk of the large white oak, the boy inched as close as he could. He didn't know when he'd see his father again or for how long.

"Your grandfather, Moyshe-Yakov Schteinkov, did what he wanted, said what he wanted, went where he wanted, ate what he wanted, and God forbid if anyone tried to stop him. He ruled Odessa, a city of enlightenment, of Jewish acceptance, literature, music, art, finance, and international intrigue. The Pale of Settlement, after all. Dozens of languages were spoken in that thriving metropolis, a gumbo of cultures, ethnicities, and religions. If you were a Jew in the late nineteenth century, Odessa was the place to be. Conceived by the brilliant Potemkin, lover to Catherine the Great, and founded in 1794 by Empress Catherine's Admiral de Ribas, Odessa was constructed on the Black Sea, where the mouths of four of the largest European rivers empty: Dnieper, Dniester, Bug, and Danube. It was a mecca for those from Asia, Africa, Europe, by land or by sea…for those seeking religious, political, and intellectual freedom."

"Were people afraid of my grandfather? Was the Fox afraid of anyone?"

"Shh. I'll tell you all about it. You'll find out."

"Now, if you wanted to be *somebody*, Odessa was the place of dreams. The fourth largest city in the Russian Empire. Only Moscow, St. Petersburg, and Warsaw were larger. Over 50 cafés served from dawn to midnight in the city of 450,00 people. Odessa's music halls performed the finest concerts. There were publishing houses that printed in multiple languages. You could see a Shakespeare play in Yiddish. Dance studios, opera houses, and theaters were teeming every night of the week. Goods and services and financial transactions took place via the Black Sea the world over, from Kiev, to Paris, to London, New York, and the Far East."

"Dad, was my grandfather *somebody*?" asked Moishie. Hope and excitement flickered in his eyes.

"Are you kidding me? He was the biggest *somebody*. Now don't interrupt," scowled Nikolai. But his son could tell there was a kind smile behind the glare.

"Now, if you wanted to lose yourself, Odessa was also the place to be. It was bursting with bakeries and butcher shops, fishmongers and money lenders. There were ship builders, giant fisheries, enormous grain factories, grand tree-lined avenues with horse-drawn and steam- powered trams."

***

For thousands of years, there has been hate and avarice and fighting and wars between people with different ideologies, different cultures, different religions. All of this led to emigrations and the moving of generations of displaced persons. This opened the door to an underworld, a place of greedy and ambitious mobsters giving way to centers for illegal substances and activities. Odessa was a global smuggling hub with powerful lords of the underworld and innumerable go-betweens, those who shuffled back and forth and did the bidding of the Fox.

***

"And you were his son, like you and me?" Nikolai hesitated, fell silent for a moment, misty-eyed.

"Yes. His only son, like you and me," said Nikolai, patting his son's knee.

"He was an influencer, and could charm a snake with a fleeting glance of those shimmering blue eyes. He was handsome with jet-black curly hair, swarthy complexion, a square jaw, a modified handlebar mustache, and a beguiling smile."

"Dad, could he really charm a snake?"

"They said so," said the father, smiling, raising his eyebrows up and down like he had just performed a magic trick. "He was ruthless and savage, smart and calculating, cutthroat yet charming, untrusting but loyal, yet there were some who would swear he was kind-hearted and fair. But heaven forbid if one found themselves on the wrong side of him. He'd fix his gaze on you… people swore his eye color changed then from azure to coal black… and it was then you would know his retribution was not far behind."

"So, what happened to the Rabbi?" asked young Moishie. He sat leaning against the old oak tree under the stars, trying to scoot closer to his father.

"I've told you that story a hundred times," said Nikolai Stein. He squinted at his only son with a loving heart but a heavy one at the same time. Moishie looked at his father like one might look at God himself if one were to see Him for the first time.

"I know, but I want you to tell me one more time," Moishie said with pleading eyes, moving a little closer in the just-short-of-chilly evening.

"OK. But this is the last time," said Nikolai, chortling, wide-eyed, raking his son close to him with his left arm so that their shoulders were squeezed together.

***

On a pleasant and warmer-than-usual October day, Moyshe-Yakov sat in a plain wooden chair, expanded chest, confirming his pride and joy at having decided to marry. In particular, to marry Esther Zoftik Petrov from Slobodka. Esther sat in a smaller, tufted chair beside him. They both sat in front of Rabbi Brodsky in his tiny office on the western wall of his Slobodka synagogue. He sat behind his worn oak table with one wobbly front leg, the table wiggling as if it might fall down at any moment. Old black leather-bound books were piled high on the right and left sides of the table surface, so that all you saw was a bibliophilic alleyway that led to the rabbi's face and upper torso. He had black piercing eyes and beefy red lips that were sandwiched between his bushy black mustache and his scraggly, graying chest-length beard.

"So, Moyshe-Yakov, to what do I owe this honor? What can I do for you?"

Now the Rabbi knew of The Fox's reputation as head of the Odessa hoodlums, and in fact he knew him from many years ago.

"Esther and I are to be married. You married my parents. And you officiated my Bar Mitzvah. We'd like you to marry us."

"I see, Moyshe-Yakov," said the Rabbi, narrowing his eyes as he looked over the wire-rimmed spectacles that just barely held to the end of his nose. He did not even glance at the bride-to-be as he shifted in his chair. His right leg, with its black shiny leather boot, clunked against the table leg nearest to him.

"Your bride-to-be is a beautiful young woman," said the Rabbi. "You are a lucky man." He would still not allow his eyes to shift toward the young woman before him. Esther had a subtle beauty. She had rich, dark-brown, wavy hair, cut short but not too short, large emerald green eyes with long lashes. Her small rose-like lips warmed her smooth facial features, and lit up her sparkling white smile when she wore bright red lipstick. Of course, sitting in front of the Rabbi, she applied no make-up and wore a plain, high-necked white cotton dress whose hem hung inches from the ground.

"And how did you two meet, may I ask?" monotone, no change in his expression.

"To tell the truth, Rabbi, Esther sings at many of the cafes in Odessa, but mostly at Café Liebman, one of the Jewish-owned cafés. She has a beautiful voice. Some say she has the finest pitch in all of Odeshchyna."

"And the girl's parents?" asked the Rabbi.

Moyshe was getting annoyed with the usual questions that would and should be asked of a new couple. And for sure, more would be coming. But Moyshe was not a patient man. And besides, he felt in his guts, in his bones, that something was a bit off.

"Her father is Pincus Daniil Petrov, a fishmonger down at the waterfront promenade, an honest, hard-working man."

"You know that I knew your father, Victor Yevghani Schteinkov?" said the Rabbi, leaning forward, now sticking his head between the two stacks of books.

"Yes, of course. As I already said, this is why we are here. You married my parents, Rabbi."

Moyshe gritted his teeth and scowled at the cleric. He wasn't used to anyone questioning him in such a manner.

"And did you know that I knew your grandfather, Schmuel Solomon Schteinkov, also?" asked the Rabbi. He pushed his glasses back on his nose, staring now with eyes like saucers at Moyshe-Yakov.

"Yes, of course, Rabbi. He was a big *macher* at the temple on Kuibysheva Street when you were the Rabbi there during my boyhood," said the groom-to-be, the muscles in his jaw tightening with each question.

"I see," said the Rabbi, stroking his beard, again knocking his right boot against the unsteady table leg.

***

"You see, Moishie, twenty years before, this Rabbi Brodsky was the spiritual leader of the Bet Israel Synagogue on Kuibysheva Street in Odessa."

"He seems mean and ugly," said the boy.

"Please, I'll never finish if you keep interrupting," said the father, knowing his son did not want the story to ever end.

***

The young rabbi came from the city of Kherson, hoping to have a long and happy position serving the religious needs of his new Odessa congregation. As a boy, Moyshe-Yakov remembered this new Rabbi Brodsky with a wooden right leg, which was hidden by his long black rabbinical robes. They said he lost it during a pogrom in the city of Kherson when he was a boy. Limping around the temple evoked somewhat of an eerie presence, especially to the young boys. Some made fun of and took every chance to run by and accidentally knock him in the dust. But the Rabbi seemed to get along with most, and fulfilled his duties with care and kindness.

There were 50 families, mostly blue-collar workers, a significant number of very poor worshippers, and of course the *alte kakkers* (old men) who began their day with the morning minyan, a quorum of ten men gathering in order to pray before our Lord. The minyan began at 6 am. Schmuel Solomon Schteinkov, Moyshe-Yakov's grandfather, being the wealthiest member of the synagogue, would drive his Mercedes-Benz, one of the first in Odessa and perhaps in all of Russia, into the poorest Jewish section of Odessa. He'd go door to door picking up ten penniless men. He would stuff them into the car and drive to the synagogue each morning. They would don their tefillin, conduct their prayer service, then participate in a breakfast of schnapps, gefilte fish, and smoked herring, all provided by Schmuel. This arrangement appeared to proceed without a hitch, until the elders realized that the Rabbi would not join these early morning supplicants. Despite promising to attend these important services over the years, the Rabbi would not negotiate this dawn service that was the essence of the beginning of each day of Jewish life.

No coaxing, cajoling, prodding, and finally demanding could get this stubborn young cleric to join this appeal for community expression and support, let alone lead the most important homage to the Almighty. The politics came to a head. The members of the board, made up entirely of the oldest congregants (led by the president Schmuel Solomon and his brother Ze'ev) threatened the Rabbi with an ultimatum: attendance at morning minyan or out. Within weeks, it became clear that the young spiritual leader had no intention of complying with their simple request. He was summarily fired. He was forced to find another congregation. A new, more compliant rabbi was hired soon thereafter.

Of course, these politics occurred when Moyshe was a boy. He had no knowledge or understanding of the past events. When he decided to get married, he simply inquired of those who might know the whereabouts of the Rabbi who married his parents and presided over his own Bar Mitzvah. Finding out the synagogue at which Rabbi Brodsky was now employed, Moyshe and his bride-to-be drove in his Model-T Ford to Slobodka. They now sat in front of the Rabbi, where Moyshe's patience was wearing thin.

"So, when were you thinking of getting married, Moyshe-Yakov?" Even a brief glance at Esther would have revealed a rosy complexion, a certain new fullness to her figure, a bit of a curve to her abdomen outlined through her loosely fitting dress. She slouched in her chair to the right of Moyshe.

"Well, we are planning to be married in mid-May, seven months from now, when the temperature is warm, the skies are blue, the winds are calm, and there's a hint of sea salt in the air."

Pausing for a moment, sighing several times, the Rabbi brought from the pocket of his robes a small brown leather-bound book wrapped with a wide leather strap and placed it in front of him on the table. He unwound the leather strap, opened the book, leafed through the pages, and sighed a few more times. He furrowed his brow while he adjusted his spectacles, and said,

"I'm sorry, Moyshe-Yakov, but I have a funeral that I must preside over in May."

Moyshe's eyebrows rose to the ceiling. His eyes bulged, straining his sockets. He glanced sharply at Esther. Moyshe gripped the arms of his chair, pushed himself forward, leaned toward the Rabbi, and said in a low growl,

"A funeral? A funeral? Did I hear you correctly? So even though our funerals must be held within twenty-four hours of one's death, you have a funeral in May? So, for that reason, you won't be able to perform the ceremony?"

"Well, what day in May were you hoping to be married?" asked the Rabbi. He didn't flinch in any way, but simply posed the question as if he were asking the young man in front of him whether he thought it would rain today.

Seeing where this was going, Moyshe was speechless. He could barely hold it together. Seething, with clenched teeth, nostrils flaring, he blurted out, "May 15th, Rabbi."

The Rabbi adjusted himself in his chair, banged his wooden leg once more against the right front table leg, and stared at his brown leather appointment book. He bent at the waist, squinted through his thick glasses, and pointed with his right index finger to a place on the page opened to him.

"Hmm. Yes. I'm sorry, but that is the exact day of the funeral in May at which I must officiate," he said calmly, apologetically, with a slight smile.

Moyshe stiffened. His face flashed scarlet. He wanted to rip this lizard's head off. He'd done it to others before. But not in front of his fiancée. He gripped the edge of the Rabbi's desk until his knuckles turned white. The wooden desk creaked beneath his fingernails. His eyes flushed bloodshot. He glanced over at Esther.

"So, Rabbi, you know who I am. You know the man I have become since you last saw me at my Bar Mitzvah. With my fiancée present to witness what you said, so it is clear to all of us here, you will not marry me and my wife-to-be, despite having married my parents, Victor Yevghani Schteinkov and Maria Galina Yankovitch. You cannot marry us in the month we have asked, nor especially the day we have requested, because you must attend a funeral on that very day in May, seven months from now."

"I'm afraid so," said the Rabbi with quiet resignation.

Fuming now with a fabricated smile from ear to ear, Moyshe seethed. "And how in God's name could you know there will be a funeral that you must attend on that day?"

"God works in mysterious ways," pronounced the Rabbi.

Without another word, Moyshe offered his hand to Esther, and the couple stormed out the door and rode home.

***

Moyshe and Esther lived happily together throughout the winter, nesting and getting ready for their wedding and their new arrival. On May fifteenth, on a beautiful day with spring washing over the port city, the happy couple were married at the old Bet Israel Synagogue amidst family and friends. Mikhail was his best man, along with Schmuel the Shark, Dmitri the Panther, H'Avram the Hammer, and Kasha the Knife. They were surrounded by music and dancing and the best food and drink in all of Odessa. Tables were set with gold rimmed dinnerware, shimmering crystal glassware, and silver cutlery. The guests dined on local beef brisket and roasted chicken, fresh goat meat and lamb kabob, bowls of bulgar and pilaf, plates of sweet kugel, seven different kinds of fish as well as caviar from their patron sea. The staff served wines from France, Italy, and Hungary, as well as oils from Greece and Turkey and Sicily. The vodka flowed like the Dnieper River, and the fun-filled festivities continued for twenty-four hours. Of course, all the guests returned home late and crashed with exhaustion. All was still in the home of the newlyweds as the sun rose the next morning.

And yet, early that morning, there came a knock, knock, knock at the door of the home of Moyshe.

"Who could be knocking so early in the morning the day following our wedding night?" said Moyshe to his new bride.

He dragged himself out of bed and wobbled to the front door. He opened the door, and Mikhail pushed his way in.

"Moskie, Moskie, did you hear? Did you hear what happened?" cried Mikhail, shoving the local newspaper in his friend's face.

"What, what? What is all the fuss about on the morning following my wedding night, my comrade?"

"In the newspaper, front page of the *Odesskiy Listok*. On the very day of your wedding, Rabbi Brodsky of Slobodka, our past rabbi, was found dead in a pool of blood in his house. He was found by his wife with his throat cut. He was slashed with a knife from gullet to zatch."

"That's awful," said Moyshe, handing the newspaper back to Mikhail. "Such a nice man."

"And the strangest thing," said Mikhail. "The newspaper said that the police found his wooden leg nailed to the lamppost outside his house, complete with his one remaining black shiny leather boot. And pinned to the upper portion of his wooden leg was a small black torn piece of cloth like those that we all wear at funerals."

"Is that so, my friend?" said Moyshe, placing his arm around the shoulder of his best man.

"God does work in mysterious ways.

Chapter 2
Alone

As a boy, Moyshe-Yakov's family home on the outskirts of the city appeared enormous, a three-story bright yellow wooden clapboard with white shutters. In the center of the expansive wrap-around porch was a green metal glider couch fitted with comfortable floral-designed cushions. There stood a group of four natural wicker armchairs surrounding a coffee table, the surface of which was made of ceramic mosaic. The five-bedroom house sat in the middle of two acres of emerald green lawn surrounded by an eight-foot hedge on three sides. The long driveway made of crushed seashells leading from Mukachevsky Street to a circular turnaround made the ten-minute walk to the ocean a bit longer.

At one end of the long porch was the entrance to a small room where Moyshe could work on his projects. In the summer, spring, and fall he would preserve and catalogue in albums the butterflies he caught with his net. Other days, he'd prepare colorful ceramic tiles for the mosaics he and his mother created together. The interior of his workroom was too cold in the winter.

At the other end of the long porch was an entrance to his father's medical office and a small patient waiting room. The main entrance to the house opened to the living room, adorned with a beautiful hemp area rug finely woven with a Moroccan design, a comfortable couch with mahogany end tables, and tufted arm chairs on either side of the large stone fireplace.

Each year, as the warm months approached, young Moyshe watched Anatoly dig and prepare the garden on the south side of the house. Anatoly said little. He was in his late fifties, small, wiry, and strong, a straw hat covering his bald head. His face was stubbled gray. His yellowing grin revealed more teeth missing than not as he tended to his duties. He was responsible for all household repairs, yard maintenance, care of the horses boarded in the barn near the house, and property protection when necessary.

"Here?" Moyshe asked. Anatoly nodded, showing the young boy over and over where to place each new plant.

"This far apart?" The little man nodded. He gestured to the doctor's son where to place the stakes for the tomatoes, how to tie the vines of the green beans as they grew, and how to attend to the snow peas climbing up the wooden lattice. He showed him how to plant the rhubarb and the strawberries around the garden's border.

***

Carrying a large wooden basket of fruits and vegetables through the kitchen door, Maria Galina Schteinkov's nine-year-old son said, "Father's going to need some of these for his patients. And the rest are for you, Mother." He was now the Keeper of the Garden, harvesting the ripened produce all summer long. Dr. Victor Yevghani Schteinkov often shared the garden yield with his patients, recommending various plant extracts for reducing premenstrual symptoms, leg cramps, back pain, and other ailments. Maria Galina cooked her cache of fresh garden delights in her large coal-burning oven. Another stove stood in the living room, providing heat for the entire house during the winter months in Odessa.

On this day, his birthday, Moyshe was excited. This afternoon he would be working with his mother on a new mosaic project, a picture to be hung in his bedroom. On a maple board, his mother inked a drawing of three horses grazing in a bucolic sun-drenched field. She was always patient with the boy. Before each project, they walked to the pottery shop to pick out various stones, different colored pieces of ceramic tile, bags of brilliant local seashells, as well as their grout mixture.

"Like this?" he asked his mother as she lovingly directed his hands on the tile cutter to form the piece that would fit.

"Here?" he asked, placing the colorful piece at just the right spot. His mother smiled and nodded at her younger son, now her only son. It was five years since her oldest child, Boris, died in the service of the tsar, an unnecessary skirmish at the bidding of Alexander III. She didn't like to think about the unbearable, the hole in her heart, at times like this. Not while she spent time with her only pride and joy.

"I heard that when your father is done with work today, he is going to take you for another riding lesson," said Maria Galina, smiling, putting her arm around her son.

"Yes, and I can't wait," said the boy, placing just the right stone to finish the horse's hoof.

***

The beaches of Odessa were known world over…white sand, soft rolling waves, bordering the southwest boundaries of the city. The warm humid drafts kept the gliding seagulls aloft, as one breathed the sea salt and the faint smell from the many fisheries at the nearby seaport. Moyshe took a swim at Arkadia Beach, smooth sand backed by the tenuous cliffs whose erosion often threatened the city's property lines. How many peaceful summer days as a boy had he spent with his parents on the shore, he thought as he walked home one springtime afternoon. The days were warming up but the nights remained cool. He was a man now. He completed his Bar Mitzvah several weeks ago. He noticed the other boys his age grew bigger, stronger, more muscular. He was small for his age, but handsome and athletic. He kept up scholastically with his colleagues at school, but he was clearly losing a step on the soccer field. On this warm June day, he planned to bridle and saddle his favorite horse, Alexei, and ride out to the forest to help Anatoly bring in a load of firewood.

Anatoly just finished chopping as Moyshe arrived. Together they stacked, bundled, and bound the wood. It was getting dark in the forest, as the young equestrian dragged his load homeward ahead of Anatoly. Tonight's emerging full moon helped lead the way.

Funny, there seemed to be a subtle tension lately at home, mimicked at school as well, mused the boy as he rode toward the house. More-than-usual whispering and laughing among the older boys. He overheard one teacher say quietly to another something about, "…those Jew merchants, and bankers, and shop owners."

Even at home, his father talked in a soft tone to his mother about instances some of his Jewish patients had to endure…shop windows smashed, butchers refusing to sell to certain families, school masters doling out punishment to select children. Ugly. Entering the barn about a week ago, he noticed Anatoly cleaning two shotguns that Moyshe had never seen.

***

As Moyshe dismounted his horse, he heard a distant crack, and then another. Gunshots? The gunfire now grew closer. Through the near darkness he saw an advancing cloud of smoke. Anatoly galloped down the drive on his horse yelling, "Get in the house! They're coming! They're raping and setting fire to everything!" Anatoly ran into the barn. He grabbed the shotguns and sprinted toward the house. Moyshe heard the sound of hoofbeats coming up the driveway. The pair reached the doctor's office and pounded on the door.

"They're coming! The mob! They're coming, Doctor! The secret police are coming!" yelled Anatoly.

Dr. Schteinkov opened the door to the sweat-stained face of his caretaker and the pale, confused face of his son. Anatoly shoved the shotgun into the doctor's hands. Hearing gunshots and loud voices outside her kitchen window, Maria Galina ran from her stove, yelling, "What's wrong? What's going on?" wiping her hands on her apron, staring into her husband's bulging eyes. Footsteps. Pounding up the stairs to the porch.

"Kill the Jews! Blow them apart! Tear them to pieces!" Lights from torches drew closer, maybe 50 yards. The boy's heart was pounding. His breathing was short. He saw frightened faces…Mother, Father, Anatoly. Tears ran down Maria Galina's face. Moyshe's father's face turned ashen.

"Hurry," cried Anatoly. "Get in the house and lock the door."

The boy stared at the guns in the hands of Victor and Anatoly. He ran for the kitchen to get the biggest knife he could find. He heard the front door close loudly. The lock clicked into place.

"Oh, my God, Victor. My boy."

A loud crash. Screams from his mother.

"Kill the traitors, the infidels."

Shots rang out. More screaming.

"My son!"

"Take me. Don't hurt my family."

Another shot rang out. Then another.

"You murderers," Anatoly screamed out.

The boy squeezed the handle of the kitchen knife. The shouting and hollering continued. A final piercing cry. Making out a flash of the monstrous gang of hyenas breaking through the front door, Moyshe twisted and turned his head, scouting the kitchen. In an instant, he targeted the oven. His lean body allowed him to squeeze behind it. He opened the metal door in the wall and crawled into the coal bin. He closed the door silently, and scrambled deeper into the pitch-black space. He sat on the black dusty piles of coal, breathing heavily, eyes closed, heart pounding, and tried to lie still.

The banging and yelling and glass breaking persisted. *There will be no end to this nightmare,* he thought as he sat with tears running down his face, sweaty and filthy in his wet, urine-stained riding pants.

Waiting…waiting until they open that door. Until they drag me out. Until they put an end to my life.

***

The boy woke with a start. Listening. The chaos had stopped. The boy waited for perhaps an hour until he opened the black metal door slowly and squeezed through the aperture. He flattened himself behind the stove and stood absolutely still. Quiet. He barely noticed the kitchen knife he clutched in his right hand. Rancid smoke wafted into the house. The kitchen floor was covered with broken glass. The cupboards were open, and two generations of dishes had been smashed. The shards crunched under his feet as he walked slowly in the near-dark from the kitchen to the living room.

The glow from the full moon revealed three bodies lying on the living room rug. His mother, father, and Anatoly were sprawled out on the floor like rag dolls. The boy stood and stared at the silent, lifeless figures who lay in pools of blood. The surrounding couches, chairs, tables, and vases were ripped and overturned and smashed.

It was not clear when the boy noticed that he was shivering. He swung hard with his right arm, sticking the knife deep into an end table. Mechanically, he walked over to the hook on the wall to the right of the front door and took down the coat and hat that hung there…soft brown leather, lambs-wool lining, and abalone buttons. A hat to match.

"Moyshe-Yakov, my son, I finished making these for you," his mother said to him.

"Wear these when you get cold. Wear them until they no longer fit you. Promise me that you will keep them always and give this hat and coat to your son."

The boy could still smell his mother's fragrance as he donned the heavy coat and hat. Did he hear a soft groan? Expressionless, he shuffled across the lawn, past the crackling barn, and down the shell driveway to the street. He slowly walked for twenty minutes, head down, barely noticing the burning houses on either side of the street. Horses, dogs, cows, and goats walked aimlessly. Women wailed while holding their infants in their arms in the cold night air. Men stood holding their children's hands and stared at the burning embers of their homes, property after property looking as if a tornado had hit. Except for the gaps where he could see no damage…the Gentile properties.

The boy stopped at a home, still standing, made of fieldstone, with two white pillars framing the entrance, and a large oak door beyond the front stairway. A crucifix was affixed to the swinging gate leading to the front walkway. He knocked and knocked until a tall, thin man opened the door. He was balding, with thick gold-rimmed glasses and a short manicured black beard. Pupils dilated, he stood aghast and stared down at the boy with a blackened face, coat half-buttoned against the chilly, smoky night air, looking as if he'd been stuffed down a chimney and fallen on the fire below.

"Moyshe-Yakov," said Dr. Sokolov, a friend and colleague of the boy's father.

"Have you walked all this way? What has happened to you? Where are your parents?" asked the physician.

"Please. Come see them," said the boy in a muffled voice.

"Yes. Of course I will, son," said the man without hesitation.

Dr. Sokolov put on his hat and coat, grabbed his medical bag, and hurried out the door. The boy stepped up onto the seat of the wagon next to the man. The doctor directed his Morgan through the ravaged section of the city until he reached 2 Mukachevsky Street. He walked with the boy past the charred barn, not wanting to look inside, though the smell of burnt animal flesh was unmistakable. Walking through the front door, he became sickened at the three dead figures near the entrance.

What kind of human beings, what kind of animals, what kind of God? he thought.

The boy laid down next to his mother in his heavy coat and hat. He closed his eyes while the doctor shifted from body to body.

I took an oath. And for what? thought the healer. He helplessly approached the bodies, moving from victim to victim, placing his second and third fingers of his right hand on their necks just below the angle of the jaw. He did not expect to find any sign of life, of course. His associate and compatriot, the mother of the boy…gracious, kind, artistic, the mangled body of the servant. He stood from a kneeling position.

No. It's my imagination, he said to himself, alone in the dark, alone in his sorrow, amidst his deep feeling of impotence. Just then, he thought he heard a soft groan from the lifeless figure. He turned the body over and placed his ear toward the mouth, a hand gently on the chest. He could detect faint breath sounds emerging from the dried, bluish lips, a slight rising and falling of the chest wall. A gaping, bloody abdominal wound through to the back was certainly made by a forceful saber blade. It was bleeding, but the rate of blood flow had diminished to a trickle. More low moaning. Taking gauze from his bag, the doctor packed the wound as best he could, picked up the flaccid body, and walked to the doorway.

"Come on, son," he heard the doctor say, the child opening his eyes wide. The healer stood there, straining with the burden in his arms.

"Hurry."

The boy stood there and shook his head in silence.

"I said we have to go," insisted Dr. Sokolov.

The boy shook his head again.

"Moyshe-Yakov, I must bring him to the hospital. Now!" The boy still did not move.

"Augh."

Holding the limp body, the doctor turned around, trudged down the porch stairs, ran across the lawn, and placed the body in the back of the wagon. He paused, looked back at the house, turned and jumped up into the wagon seat. He snapped the reins and galloped toward the hospital. Back at the house, the boy lay back down and curled up next to Maria Galina, closed his eyes, his heart full of sadness and fury. Fighting it, fighting it, fighting it, he finally fell off to sleep.

When the boy awoke near dawn, he rose from the floor, filled the living room stove to the hilt with coal and kindling. He reached for a match and lit the stove, as his father had taught him. He opened the flue so that the flames would roar as they did in mid-winter. Leaving the burning stove door wide open, he already could see the sparks flying from the roaring fire onto the hemp rug. The boy turned from the stove, his heart breaking, but at the same time straining from the weight of a protective steel covering that was rapidly forming around the center of his soul. He walked out of the house, down the endless drive, and set out on the long walk to the hospital.

Chapter 3
Survival

Moyshe sat by the wounded man's bedside day after day. The boy had no one. Anatoly Yuri Petrovsky was the only adult at number 2 Mukochevsky Street to survive the pogrom. The ailing man smiled at the doctor's son, but remained in a weakened state for weeks. The young man, mentally shell shocked, offered small talk, and bits of encouragement. Mostly, he sat and stared. The family caretaker looked small and skinny in the bed. Sallow skin, motionless, he slept most of the day and night. Each night, the boy dozed on the edge of Anatoly's cot. Natalya Oksana, Anatoly's wife, visited each day, but not before she completed her work. She laundered the filthy garments of others, mostly the wealthy. This earned her a meager sum. Someone had to bring in some rubles.

She looked older than her 50 years… graying unkept hair, overweight, fallen arches, loose skin that waved below her triceps, but she was physically strong and mentally tough. The boy thought her to be kind, honest, and dutiful. Natalya brought Moyshe a bowl of thin soup, or a piece of goat meat, or a chicken bone, barely enough to sustain him as he sat with the man who had spent his life supporting and protecting him and his family.

The old man finally recovered enough from his near-mortal injuries to be released from the hospital. The boy was glad to be taking him home. Anatoly leaned on the young thirteen-year-old. They walked back to Mulavanka, near the seaport, the poorest district of the city. Of course, Natalya insisted on Moyshe coming to live with them. Where else was he to go? The still-injured, frail, unshaven man leaned on Moyshe as the boy led him down the crowded, foul-smelling streets, lined by rows of eight-story brick tenement houses, wild dogs and rodents running past as they shuffled along. Shirts, dresses, undergarments and rags hung from the clotheslines strung between the building windows.

Anatoly finally stopped at a street-level doorway, white paint peeling off the wooden frame. Down a few stairs, they entered a single room, with a small bed, an old wood/coal-burning stove, and a tin bowl atop a waist-high cabinet. A thin pine-wood bench, perhaps six feet, stood at the opposite wall. A large jar of soap cakes sat next to a wooden wash basin on the floor. Eight clotheslines hung along the ceiling, from one wall to the opposite about two feet apart. A small wire bird cage with one blue and one green parakeet hung from the far corner. Moyshe spied several rats running across the dirty floor as they entered.

"Welcome home. I made some nice potato soup," said Natalya. The three sat down at a wooden table for two and ate the thin, tasteless soup in silence. No forks. No knives. No napkins or glassware. Anatoly slumped at the table with his eyes closed, his soup only half-eaten. Night was approaching.

"Finish this," said Natalya. "You'll be hungry." Moyshe finished what little soup was left. His stomach still rumbled.

Bedtime came soon after supper. Natalya took Moyshe's clothes, including his hat and coat, and promised to clean them in the morning. She handed him a torn night-shirt. All three climbed into the small bed with Moyshe sandwiched in the middle. Anatoly immediately began to snore. Moyshe faced the back of Natalya, who slept in her cotton nightgown. She was large and sweaty, with pendulous breasts and spreading buttocks. The moth-eaten blanket smelled like body odor. Natalya smelled rancid and Anatoly smelled worse.

"Good night, Moyshe-Yakov," said Natalya, turning her head and smiling at him with a toothless grin. "You are welcome for as long as you like. Try to sleep if you can."

In the dark, no one could see the tears streaming down his cheeks.

This will not be my fate, he thought to himself, yet he was thankful for the kindness shown to him.

***

A teenage boy, at the turn of the century, lost in a sprawling international melting pot, where the rug gets pulled out from under him, riches to rags, falling through a hole in the earth, Moyshe would wake up each morning thinking, *What's for breakfast?* Each night, *Anything for dinner?*

He spent his days walking down at the seaport where ships delivered and received produce, machinery that powered the industry of the nation, and textiles, leather goods, art and jewelry that powered its vanities and egos. He'd walk through Privoz Market where wagons were weighed down with fresh water elder, apples, potatoes and mushrooms, spices and herbs, nuts and grains, wines and vodka, fish and meats of all kinds. Anatoly was still recovering from his near-death experience and required continued care. He certainly could not work. Though Natalya scrubbed clothes from dawn to dusk, it soon became clear that after rent, washing supplies and extortion fees, there was no money left for food, never mind other needs. Moyshe-Yakov had never lived with hunger. Not really. He looked desperately at the rats that scampered about. *No…he couldn't. He wouldn't.*

***

Fall moved on toward winter. Winter graduated to Spring. There would be no graduating for Moyshe. He had abandoned school. *For what? For him to become a target? To learn mathematics? To grasp the scientific questions and answers of the universe? Fuck it. He was hungry.*

The gatherings of pigeons in Venice's St. Mark's Square, or Dbrovnik's Luza Square, or Krakow's Main Market Square were well known, and so too these city birds settled in flocks in Teatralnaya Square, in front of the Odessa Opera and Ballet Theatre. One early summer afternoon, as he walked up from the docks with a loaf of bread under his arm that had fallen off a cart, Moyshe could not believe that he hadn't thought of this possible feast in waiting.

He put his plan into action. While the others were sleeping, he rose pre-dawn in the darkness from the hard bench that was his bed. He walked on his toes toward the jar in which Natalya kept seed for the parakeets, and borrowed a handful. He walked in the dark up to the square where the pigeons gathered in strength. He removed his coat, threw a few seeds on the ground and the birds moved toward him, triggering a childhood memory.

"Grandma. Grandma. How did you get this magnificent specimen? It is by far the biggest in my entire butterfly collection."

"I was walking near Sobornaya Square with your parents last evening under the street lamps, and I saw something move on the ground. I thought it was a frog, so I threw my sweater over it, for you. When I brought it home and unwrapped my sweater, I was surprised at the expansive wings, the colorful eyespots, and the tainted crescent streaks toward the body."

"It's called a Samia Cynthia moth, Grandma."

As the pigeons feasted on the seeds, Moyshe threw his coat over them…to no avail. The prey all scattered, evading the ill-conceived plan. Over and over the boy tried and failed until he ran out of seeds. Shoulders slumped, he walked home. The pigeons won. He lost. He tried and failed over the next three nights.

Strangely, each night as Moyshe trudged toward his hunt, a boy his age, a little shorter, blond hair, muscular build, passed him going the opposite way. Most nights this competitor passed him with a string of pigeons slung over his shoulder. The dead pigeons, four or five, hung from the string like fish on a line after a good day's catch. He whistled as he walked by in the dawn light, side-glancing at Moyshe-Yakov. Then with a smirk, he'd break into a jaunt.

Finally, on the fifth evening, Moyshe was rewarded with one brown pigeon that he quickly grabbed from beneath his coat and shoved into his pocket. He ran home and showed it to Natalya.

"You want me to cook that thing? Absolutely not. You kill it and defeather it first. Then I'll cook that scrawny bird."

It took him hours, no...days, to catch one bird. Meanwhile, he picked up as many coal pieces as he could that day as they fell off the passing carts, and collected them in an old pail. He planned for the fire they would need to cook his catch. Moyshe then sat on the stoop for the rest of the day, getting hungrier and hungrier, but unwilling to kill the bird in his pocket. Around 6 pm when Natalya finished her washing, he thought to himself, *We'll either have nothing to eat tonight, or fish soup with no fish in it.*

He grabbed the bird out of his pocket, at first loosely, but it almost flew away. Squeezing tighter, he closed his eyes and twisted mightily.

CRACK. Opening his eyes, he saw the lifeless form slumped in his hand. He plucked the feathers but quickly came the admonishment, "Hey you. You and your feathers. Move away from the doorway. You're going to mess up the place." He completed his mission down the street, brought the bird into their hovel, and gave it to Natalya.

"Thank you," she said with a smile but strangely at the same time with eyes that seemed sad.

"You're a good boy. I'm sorry that I can't provide what you need. I'll cook this for us tonight."

"You know, Moyshe-Yakov, I grew up on a farm in Deribasovka, a town about 5 miles outside Odessa. We were poor but I never knew we were poor. My mother sewed all of my and my sister's clothes. We had our chores. My father worked the fields and provided for us as best he could. I never thought I would be anything but a simple working girl. I met Anatoly because his father had a small neighboring farm. Anatoly used to deliver produce to your grandfather. Mr. Schteinkov was impressed with Anatoly and hired him on the spot to maintain his property."

"It must have been rough for you at times."

"Oh, not that I didn't have dreams. Say, did you know that parakeets can live fifteen years or longer? I swore that if I ever got free, free to go and come and buy and eat whatever I wanted, I would liberate those birds as a symbol of my freedom from all this." She pointed to their rat-infested home.

The next night he returned to the square, earlier, around midnight. He proceeded cautiously, and crouched quietly behind a tree. He watched until he noticed movement under the street lamp. It was the blond boy with a string in his hand. The string was attached to a stick some thirty feet away. The stick held up one end of an old wooden milk crate. On the ground were seeds leading under the box that six pigeons were pecking at when…SNAP. The boy yanked the string toward him. The crate slammed down as two pigeons flew away. The kid ran over to the crate, stuck his hand underneath, and pulled out four pigeons one by one. As he grabbed each bird, he twisted its neck, and knotted it onto the string. He placed the stick into the crate and carried it behind a series of thick bushes bordering the square. The boy walked away with the string of dead pigeons over his shoulder. Moyshe watched and marveled until the young man was out of sight.

Assuring himself that the master trapper had gone, Moyshe returned home. He quietly removed the longest clothesline, marched back up to the square, retrieved the crate and stick, and copied the technique he had just witnessed. He strung up his catch, replaced the crate and stick in their hiding place and walked home. He prepared his six-bird reward.

"Oh my. You're not only getting bigger and stronger but craftier I see," said Natalya, taking the birds and placing them on the stove the next morning.

Over the next several months, he collected daily bits of coal and foraged for firewood in the forests within the many parks and gardens of Odessa. Natalya happily cooked his ornithologic triumphs. Meanwhile his eyes adjusted to a new world. He hated the man who hounded Natalya for his extortion money "to keep your home and family and livelihood safe." As a street-smart teenager, he was acutely aware of the haves…fine French and Italian clothes, sleek houses set upon the cliffs overlooking the Black Sea, even automobiles…and the have-nots… living in squalor not knowing from where their next meal would come.

***

Walking up Gamannaya Street one day the following Spring, climbing up from the city harbor, he saw a horse pulling a cart carrying a fisherman's bounty. The horse suddenly reared up, again and again, whinnying at a high pitch. Out of the corner of his eye, he noticed a snake lying curled up beneath the pounding hooves. The cart slanted up and down, and with this, a crate of Black Sea bass slipped off the cart and onto the street. Reacting instinctively, hungrily, the athletic Moyshe darted behind the cart, picked up the fallen crate, turned and ran. Just as he turned, he saw the Pigeon Boy standing there with a scowl.

"Hey, that's mine," yelled the boy, brandishing his fist. With the cart driver screaming obscenities, Moyshe ran all the way home with his new-found sea treasure. Just as he returned home, he heard from behind, "That's minc. Give it back," said Pigeon Boy, standing there arrogantly with hands on his hips.

"Who says?" panted Moyshe, still breathing heavily from the run home.

"Finders keepers, losers weepers."

"But I set it up," contested the blond boy.

Moyshe raised his eyebrows, his head tilted to one side, a thousand gears clicking into place in his mind. His ears moved back a bit. He dropped the crate of fish on the ground and turned to the boy.

"Listen, whatever-your -name-is, what do you mean you set it up?"

"My name is Mikhail-Simon. I scared the horse to rear, to upset the cart, so the fish would fall off the back. And who are you, anyway? Now give me my fish," said the defiant boy. He stepped closer, chin advancing, chest expanded.

"How did you set it up?"

"Easy. I painted a thick old rope, gave it a twirl, and laid it down in front of the oncoming horse and cart. You saw what happened. Horses are scared to death of snakes."

Moyshe stepped in front of the crate of fish, eyes three-quarters closed. He stared at the boy.

"My name is Moyshe-Yakov. I will not give you your fish, but let me tell you what I will do." Arms crossed in front of his chest, he lifted his chin skyward. He had grown bigger and stronger and faster over the last year on the streets. He was neither afraid nor intimidated. On the contrary, he was impressed.

"I will split the fish with you. Half for you and half for me," said Moyshe, grinning.

"Oh yeah," the other boy said slowly, cautiously. "OK, let's count," said Mikhail-Simon with eyebrows raised, nodding his head slightly, a smirk on his face that looked like it was about to turn into a grin.

The boys emptied the crate onto the steps leading to Anatoly's first floor tenement.

"…twenty-three, twenty-four, twenty-five," said Mikhail-Simon, looking up at the new boy.

"So, who gets the thirteenth fish?" asked Mikhail-Simon. He straightened up, nose to almost nose (Moyshe was two inches taller), and with a snarl, looked straight into his co-conspirator's eyes.

Again, Moyshe thought just for an instant, but in that moment calculated the past, present, and future.

"You do, of course," Moyshe smiled. Mikhail-Simon, without another word, packed the thirteenth fish into the crate, lifted it up, turned and walked away.

"Maybe I'll see you down by the docks tomorrow morning," yelled Moyshe-Yakov.

He collected his fish and brought them in to show Natalya and Anatoly. No questions asked, they thanked their adopted young man for the bounty of eight fish. Moyshe-Yakov sold the other four fish to a fishmonger down the street. He loved the sound of rubles jingling in his pocket as he walked home to a fish dinner.

Chapter 4
An Alliance

The next morning the two young men found each other at the Odessa seaport. It was a busy, bustling, loud, international port. The harbor teemed with sailors, dock workers, and merchants buying and selling a plethora of goods and services. From wharf to wharf the air was filled with varying aromas –from coffee beans in burlap bags, to earthy fragrances from barrels of sunflower oil, to pungent odors of imported horses and cattle. They stood in envy of the horse-drawn carts that picked up and delivered goods bound for the five continents….sunflower seeds and oil, corn, iron ore, coal, timber, and wheat leaving on ships to Spain, Turkey, Italy, Netherlands, Egypt, Indonesia, and China. They heard the banging and clanging of the ship builders at the far end of the seaport. They watched the vessels unloading products ranging from fabrics, furs, shoes, farm machinery, paintings, animals, jewels, and more.

The young men began to discuss survival techniques.

"So, you use a rope," said Moyshe, in a judging tone, looking out to sea, not meeting the eyes of his new compatriot.

"Yeah. It doesn't always work though."

"In another life, I used to ride horses. Did you know that besides snakes, horses are afraid of lions, wolves, and alligators? But in a more practical way, they are often afraid of cats, dogs, loud noises, honking horns, and even butterflies."

"Huh. Sounds like you know a lot about horses…and butterflies."

Days grew into weeks and months of scheming and planning. The two compadres took note of the dockyard comings and goings as well as the shipping and receiving schedules. They memorized which ships docked with certain goods, at what times, and familiarized themselves with who ran the delivery routes in town.

As their relationship grew, Moyshe learned that Mikhail also lost his parents, sisters, and brothers in the 19th century Russian pogroms. He was fifteen. He now lived with a poor aunt one street over from Natalya and Anatoly's flat. His aunt eked out a meager living as a seamstress.

"We weren't rich but we weren't poor either. When I went to live with my Aunt Sasha, I stopped going to school. School and I were like oil and water. I did well on the soccer field, the gym, ice skating, but the classroom was not for me."

"Did you play an instrument?"

"For a time, when my parents could afford it, I took piano lessons and was quite good until I had to stop. That was something that I loved."

"I, too, loved music as a boy."

Moyshe-Yakov wiggled from cheek to cheek on the piano bench while his mother played. Legs swinging, shoulders twisting, his mind focused on the melodies, the crisp notes hanging in the air like a fog settling in, smoothly surrounding the two of them, softly, gently. She stopped for a moment and turned to her son.

"I see that you have been practicing your piano in earnest lately."

"Oh, yes," said the boy. "I'm getting better and my teacher said that he thinks I'm good."

"Oh, my son, you are better than good. Some at the academy have said you are a young virtuoso."

"What does that mean?"

"It means that you should keep practicing," she smiled. "And I love to hear you play."

Moyshe-Yakov's mother turned back to her keyboard and continued to play Beethoven's Concerto No.5 in E flat (Emperor), not half as well as her mother, or her mother before her.

***

Mikhail's Aunt Sasha was in her late thirties, straight blonde hair down to her mid-back that she most often wore pinned up on top of her head. She had high cheek bones, fair skin, a Roman nose, and sparkling emerald green eyes. She was a seamstress, a young widow, having lost her husband, a fisherman shot by the Russian police when he refused to give up half of his catch of the day. Her one daughter died at eight years old of an infection she developed as a result of a dog bite. The hospital refused to treat her daughter because Sasha had no money to pay for the services required.

Sasha provided food, barely, and basic shelter for Mikhail but nothing more. Mikhail had to fend for himself. He would try to please his aunt, make her happy, but times were tough. As his teenage years rolled forward, Mikhail clearly enjoyed her smile, her lips, her shapely figure, but he kept these thoughts to himself. Let's face it, who did he really have to share such thoughts with, until now?

The boys developed a strong bond, enemies to rivals to friends maybe. Both had lost their parents, their families, their possessions in the pogroms. Their hopes and dreams? Who knew? The message they received was, *you're not wanted here.* Maybe not anywhere? Right or wrong, they felt the world owed them. And if the world was not going to give them what they deserved, they'd damn well take it.

Months went by and the two companions enjoyed increasing success in scrounging. One would frighten a mare with perhaps a hand-held horn, or a cat suddenly thrown, and the other collected the produce, the vegetables, clothing, shoes, and more as the carts would heave up and down or even overturn completely. They'd keep some of the booty but would sell most to vendors at the city market...sometimes even selling the goods back to the same merchant they'd stolen from in the first place. They adopted the name Lion Brothers. Not surprisingly they felt eyes increasingly on them...eyes of the law, eyes of the duped merchants, eyes of their competitors.

Of course, their heists were not all successful. An episode occurred where they thought the haul was one of fresh meat destined for several high-end butcher shops. As they ran away with their newfound crate of tenderloins, the strong, limber young hoodlums heard whining and barking from within. A short, seriously overweight cart driver, brandishing his fist, yelled out to them, "Hey. Come back here," and ran after the two young crooks. Up and down hills, through the tree lined streets of Odessa, around Odessa City Garden, and across Sobornaya Square. Their pursuer's breathing grew heavier and heavier and soon found himself further and further behind. He stopped and brandished his fist.

"You'll be sorry, you punks. The Wolf won't let you get away with this."

Did Moyshe see a gun in his hand? Not sure.

Meanwhile, the boys were sweating and straining under the weight of the stolen load. Carrying the barking crate, they ducked into an alley.

"What the hell?" said Mikhail. "I've never heard of tenderloins that cry, and yelp, and bark."

"Me neither," said Moyshe, brow furrowed, while he opened the crate by springing the latch. There, in the bottom of the crate, standing and sitting and whining and barking, were a half dozen puppies…black, miniature poodles.

"Holy shit," they both said in unison. They closed the crate and sat down on top of it, exhausted, chests still heaving from their escape.

"Hey, who was that guy following us?" asked Mikhail.

"Not sure, but I have a suspicion."

"Well, I hope Mr. Ageloff down at the pet store will pay good money for these fuckin' puppies."

Moyshe already forgot about the poodles. His mind was racing, thinking about their pursuer, flipping through the possibilities, weighing the implications of the threat the fat man screamed out.

***

Months later, on a hot, sunny day in August, the pair stood at the corner of Bazarnaya and Osipova Streets, ready and in position. They knew their target. They knew the take. Moyshe gently unscrewed the punctured metal top to the large glass jar he was holding. As the driver steered his horse and wagon around the corner, Moyshe jumped out, fully removed the top to the container and thirty-odd butterflies flew out, right in front of the unsuspecting dapple-gray mare. She jolted, raised up on her hind legs, and bucked. Ears back, bulging eyes, she ninny'd at a high pitch, racing away down Bazarnaya Street. But not before the wagon had slanted upwards at a steep enough angle enough to dump two cases of wine onto the street. One case upended and most of the bottles within were broken, spreading their red stain across both sides of the street. Mikhail ran to the second case, and standing in the pool of sticky red alcohol, grabbed the fully intact case of wine, and ran all the way home to Privoznaya Street. Soon after, Moyshe came running up to his sweaty, flushed "brother lion" who was still panting and coughing and wheezing from the long run home with the heavy prize. They looked at each other. They laughed uncontrollably, so hard that they were bent over, sides aching, until they both turned around, looked up, only to see a frightening sight...one of the scariest human beings they had ever laid eyes on... Ivan the Wolf.

Ivan Grigor Rabinovitch, otherwise known as Ivan the Wolf, or simply The Wolf, was the head of the Jewish Russian criminal underworld of Odessa. He stood six feet, five inches tall, was husky and rotund, pushing three-hundred and fifty pounds easily. His limbs were thick as a fully-grown cherry tree. He sported jet-black curly hair, a slightly trimmed mustache and beard that made his large head look like a lion's atop the body of a gorilla. When he rarely smiled, his teeth revealed his four top incisors to be bright white and longer than normal. His upper and lower canines were even bigger, all coming to a razor-sharp point.

The young robbers stood in silence, tongue-tied, mouths agape, sweat pouring down their faces. Rabinovitch, quicker than you'd think for such a large man, pushed Mikhail-Simon to the side and jumped behind Moyshe-Yakov. He grabbed him by the neck like a butcher would hold a fowl to be slaughtered and pressed a long knife to his extended neck just below his chin. The boy could smell the giant's rancid odor.

"I'm only going to say this once. You chickens now work for me. Any jobs that get done go to me. I will pay you what I want and you will take it. Understood?"

Trouble breathing, Moyshe squeezed out, "Yes. Okay, Wolf. We'll do anything you say."

"Mr. Wolf," Ivan Rabinovitch growled, tightening his grip.

"Yes, Mr. Wolf," said Mikhail. "Sir."

Just then, a Model A Ford pulled up and a wiry little man came scampering out. He grabbed the case of wine, ran and shoved it carefully into the car, and climbed behind the steering wheel. The Wolf jumped in and they drove away.

***

The Lion Brothers continued their thieving ways. They extorted businesses and homes, both rich and poor...all for The Wolf. They might receive 5 to 10 percent of the take, usually less. Most of Moyshe's money would go to Natalya and Anatoly. They were grateful for his generosity and always thanked him, no questions asked. Natalya tried to improve the comfort and décor by getting Moyshe his own cot.

Months passed. They evaded a number of close calls with the police. The gray-coated secret police would like nothing better than to jail the two Jew-boys. But the bigger fish? The Wolf? No way. He was untouchable. He was too rich, too powerful, and owned too many officials.

"I know that we are better off than we were," complained Mikhail. "And I also know that no one in Odessa could ever challenge The Wolf. But Moyshe, we take all the risk and that gorilla gets all of the reward. We're not getting any younger. We're not teenage kids anymore. It's a new century."

"I know. I know," said Moyshe. "But, my Lion Brother, I have a plan. I've been working on it for a while now. There is timing involved. Sit with me. I will tell you the details."

Chapter 5
Working for The Wolf

Moyshe loved the feel of the wad of banknotes in his right front pocket. He and Mikhail had worked for The Wolf for nearly three years. The Lion Brothers were now bigger, more mature and more experienced…nearly twenty years old. They were The Wolf's number one team. They brought in the most money, the most produce, and had a reputation for not only being thorough in their pursuits, but for being untouchable by the authorities. While high-end merchants, shipowners, and people of means might fear them, the neighborhood workers and common folk often felt protected by them. They felt safe from the competing gangs that prowled the city. The Lion Brothers contributed often to the local synagogues, alms houses, and cafés.

The Wolf asked the Lion Brothers to take on his more difficult heists, while leaving the more petty jobs to others in his crew. He met them down at the Café Libman one afternoon in early October.

"Listen. I need you guys to do a job. The other guys tried to do it. They couldn't. It's Meyer Snitkoff. Hardware merchant. Trying to stiff us. Something about a cat."

The next afternoon, Mikhail came running to Moyshe down at the promenade surrounding the seaport as he was talking to his favorite sea captain, Captain Peter Zoronsky. Mikhail's face had four huge scratches on both cheeks and blood was running down. His shirt was ripped to shreds and both trouser legs were torn badly, revealing his bloody thighs.

"Oh, my God! What the hell happened to you?" asked Moyshe.

"I went to take care of that little matter at that hardware store. There's a big cat there that sits in front protecting the store."

"And you're afraid of a little pussy?"

"This ain't no little pussycat."

"And you let a little kitten do this to you? Give me a break."

"Go see for yourself. Why don't you do the fucking job?"

"I guess I'll have to."

The next day Moyshe walked downtown to Meyer Snitkoff's hardware store. The owner was refusing to pay his extortion fee and apparently every time that Ivan the Wolf's guys tried to collect, they failed. As Moyshe approached the store, leaning against the outside wall, he saw rakes, shovels, scythes, axes, sledgehammers and other tools. What he also saw, sitting on an old weather-beaten arm chair in front of the entrance to the store, was a huge Calico cat. Gigantic. The biggest cat he had ever seen, the size of a Rottweiler. It had huge razor-sharp claws the size of a brown bear, and it began hissing and spitting as he approached. He turned around and walked home. He had an idea.

Moyshe spent the next several hours catching four rats in the neighborhood. He placed the rats one by one in a burlap sack. He cinched the bag closed and walked back to the hardware store. He glared at the cat with mustard-colored rings encircling his body. Bag in hand, Moyshe wrapped his coat around his arm and slowly approached the feline. With lightning speed, the cat reached out with its right front paw and swiped at the approaching assailant. Moyshe instinctively reacted and blocked the attack with his left arm cloaked in his coat. He stepped back just in time. He heard a ripping sound as the cat tore a large gash near the pocket all the way through to the lining and down to the outer right hem of the coat. Scowling, lips curled, now eyes black as coal, Moyshe loosened the tie atop the bag ever so slightly, just enough so the first rat stuck the tip of his whiskered nose out of the opening. He then threw the sack directly in front of the cat. In a flash, the cat jumped down off the chair and swatted the bag between its paws. In a split second, the cat dug into the bag, ripped the bag to shreds, and impaled the rats, two in each paw. As he was about to wolf them down whole…CRASH. Moyshe came crashing down with a sledgehammer, smashing the cat's skull, brains spreading in a ten-foot radius.

Moyshe eyed the owner standing in the doorway. The young cat slayer brushed past Meyer Snitkoff into the hardware store, still holding the sledgehammer.

"Monsieur," he said, motioning toward the front door. "If you don't want your intellect spread over the same area as your pussycat out there, you'd better hand over the money you owe us, plus twenty percent interest."

Stunned, hands shaking, the merchant went into the till, pulled out five hundred rubles plus twenty percent vig he owed and handed it to the young hoodlum. Moyshe drew the sledgehammer over his shoulder and feigned a swing toward the owner. Snitkoff screamed, "Please don't," and cowered to the floor. Moyshe walked out of the store and replaced the bloody sledgehammer. He met Mikhail at the corner, told him to deliver the money due The Wolf, and walked home with the twenty percent vig in his pocket.

***

On the way home from the hardware store that evening he bought a fresh loaf of brown pumpernickel, a large wedge of Havarti cheese, and a ten-pound sea bass with the last of his money. While Moyshe shared what little money he had and the occasional produce he acquired with his adopted parents, things were still quite bleak in their one-room hovel. Natalya still toiled away at her laundry business and Anatoly, who never quite recovered physically or mentally from the attack, helped his loving wife with her chores. But tonight was different.

After finishing the best dinner they had in years, Moyshe laid back on his own cot and breathed a huge sigh. He looked up at the ceiling, beams bending and cross boards gray and cracking.

Mikhail is right, he thought to himself. *Where am I going? There is better than this. I barely remember, but I do remember.*

He developed a plan and discussed it with Mikhail. He lay there finalizing the strategy, head propped up on his rolled-up coat, the torn coat he had used to protect himself from the cat attack at the hardware store. He was too big for the coat and hat that he'd been wearing for years now. The hat rested above him on a rusty nail banged into the wall. The coat had gotten old and frayed, the lining was now ripped. His head tossed and turned, thinking of the plan, the next step, the way out.

Natalya and Anatoly had been so kind. They were loving in their own way. Never judging him. Giving…but what did they really have to give?

Moyshe felt something pressing into his scalp as he adjusted the coat beneath his head. Maybe the buttons, but as he reached along the torn, discolored, lamb's wool lining, he felt something hard, the size of a Brazil nut. He dug further, along the hem. There was a loose thread. He sat up with the coat in his lap and pulled on the loose black thread. Something fell out onto the floor, hit hard and stopped rolling just under his cot. He grabbed a match, lit it, and looked under the bed. There, without a doubt, was a roundish, clear, cut gem stone. He picked it up, felt it in his hand, lit another match and stared. "Not possible. Quartz?" He looked closer, then shouted out in the dark. "A diamond? How could this be?" he said to himself. In the dark, he laid back down on his cot, gripping the stone in hand.

"Keep this coat and hat always. In time, you will give it to your son," his mother had directed.

He laid in the dark, feeling the rest of his coat hem…one, two, three lumps separated equidistantly along the bottom of the coat. His heart was pounding. Thoughts were whirling through his head like a spinning cartwheel. Excitement, confusion, exhilaration, a heaviness in his chest…his breathing was rapid. He jumped up and grabbed the hat hanging above him. As he felt the old worn headband, he fingered three equidistant cherry-sized hard shapes that he had not appreciated before. They were inches from the buttons that adorned the circumference of the hat.

I'll wait. I'll wait until tomorrow. In the light. Alone. I will keep this to myself for now.

He placed the hat back on the hook and carefully rolled the coat upon itself and placed it behind his head as he laid back down.

He couldn't sleep. He rolled the stone over and over in one hand, then switched hands and did the same. A kaleidoscope of thoughts and feelings came quickly. Too many. He waited. Waited for dawn to come. For the sun to rise over the Black Sea. The pinks and purples and feathery clouds. Over the sea that surrounded his city. The sea whose horizon spoke of places far from Odessa, the only place he had ever known.

Chapter 6
The Wolf Sets Sail

Two months had elapsed since Moyshe found the treasures in his hat and coat. The Lion Brothers knew every merchant and business in Odessa as Moyshe forged daily arrangements with merchant mariners, dock workers, as well as sailing vessel crews and steamship captains. Under the not-so-watchful eye of The Wolf, the partners shared equally in 100 percent of the profits of these new deals.

They finalized their plan. The time came one early fall afternoon, when the Lion Brothers targeted a wagon loaded with a dozen crates of the finest vintage Bessarabian red wine from the Purcari vineyards. As they hijacked the wagon in their usual fashion, the frightened driver ran off yelling, "Please don't kill me." He was well aware now of the reputation the hoodlums had gained over the last several years regarding anyone who dared to resist them. The Lion Brothers climbed up into the wagon. Moyshe grabbed the reins, and drove across town toward the home of Ivan Rabinovitch.

The Wolf grew up in an orphanage in the industrial town of Koreston. He learned his trade on the streets of Odessa. He never married. He had no children nor any living relatives in southern Ukraine. He lived alone except for his eight black toy poodles from France who roamed the premises at will. Two stone pillars and a tall black wrought iron gate opened to a winding driveway covered in crushed marble stones. The driveway led to a large estate of white-painted brick, a turret on each wing, arched windows, vaulted ceilings, wall murals and tiled floors. There was a winding staircase to the second floor, and an expansive veranda, overlooking the cliff, reaching out toward Otrada Beach and the Black Sea below. The entire three acres of lawn were bordered by mature acacia trees. As they drove the burdened horse-drawn cart up to the front of the mansion, they smelled the fragrances of lilacs, gardenias, and jasmine that weaved between the hedges of honeysuckle.

"I'm going in," said Moyshe.

Mikhail jumped down, walked toward the gate, gave a wave, and said, "Good luck, brother. I'll see you down at the docks. I'll talk to Captain Peter and make sure he gets paid."

Hearing a loud knock, The Wolf opened the front door. Moyshe stood before him with a crate of red wine. Towering over the young man, Ivan saw a wagon behind him loaded down with similar crates. The Wolf stared at Moyshe, rubbed his black whiskers and said,

"What are you doing here?"

"We have obtained a cache' of a dozen crates of the finest Bessarabian red wine. I know such wine is a favorite of yours. I thought you and I would celebrate the anniversary of when Mikhail and I started working for you. A profitable arrangement for you. No?"

"Yes, I suppose so. Come in," The Wolf said slowly, squinting at his infrequent and unannounced visitor.

"Take the crate through to the other side of the house and place it on the table on the veranda."

Moyshe strode through the beautifully appointed house… high ceilings, tapestries adorning the walls, intricate tiling covering the floor, and yapping, yapping, yapping of the eight black toy poodles, nipping at his heels. He deposited the crate on the table and stared out at the ocean, a calm breeze coming off the water, the sky nearing sunset.

"Sit," said the huge man, pointing to a chair at the table.

Moyshe sat down and nonchalantly produced two wine goblets, one smaller than the other, placing the smaller one in front of Ivan Grigor and the larger one in front of himself. The Wolf grabbed a bottle from the crate, uncorked it, and looked at the young hoodlum out of the corner of his eye. He switched glasses, and poured himself wine in the larger goblet and some for his guest. As the sun dropped below the horizon, The Wolf clicked his glass with Moyshe and said, "To another good year."

"Yes. *L'chaim.*"

They downed their wine in a few gulps, the first of many glasses. Nodding in approval, The Wolf said, "As a matter of fact, you and

Mikhail have done a good job for me. I was thinking of raising your take from five to ten percent."

"We would appreciate that, sir," smiled the young man.

As the night sky grew darker, they talked about new schemes, better opportunities...perhaps expanding their territory, purchasing several ships, establishing an import/export business. Moyshe matched The Wolf swallow for swallow. Two bottles led to three, to four, to five until there was only one bottle left.

"Thish ish surefinewine an' you have fine ideerz," slurred The Wolf, slumping over the table.

"But I have to show you my best idea," said Moyshe, steady as ever.

"Wha? Nooowww? T'nite?"

"Yes. You have to see it to believe it. And time is of the essence. The opportunity will be lost if we don't take advantage of it tonight."

"Wel'ish it far 'aray? We are not in very goo' shape t'go far?"

"No. Just a short walk down Prebodsky Street and then at the bottom of Potemkin steps. This will make you rich. I will help you, my friend. C'mon."

"Thish will make me risshh?"

"Very rich."

Moyshe grabbed The Wolf by the arm, led him past the French poodles, out the front door, and walked arm and arm with him down Prebodsky Street into the cool and quiet night air. They arrived at the Potemkin Stairs. It was tough enough to climb up the one-hundred-ninety-two steps constructed in 1837 that were the formal entrance to the city from the sea, but this attempt to go down, at night, after consuming a crate of wine, was a challenge that Moshye was well aware of. The Wolf stumbled and tripped, groaned when he fell twice, and rolled down most of the of stone steps. He somehow managed the struggle and stood at the bottom. The seaport was quiet, with only a few dock workers milling about. The most activity was near the bow of a large ship, *The Chinois*, where Moyshe barely spotted in the moonlight, his friend Captain Peter on board, waving both arms in a "hurry up" gesture.

"Almost there," said Moyshe. "This is what I wanted to show you."
"Oh, rrealy. I'm gong t' be risshh?"
He led the wobbly Ivan to the dock in front of Captain Peter's ship. Stacked three and four high were newly made wooden coffins, approximately three hundred all together.
"Look. Look, Ivan. Inside. What do you see?" asked Moyshe. He lit a match and asked The Wolf to peer into an open casket piled on top of three others.
Unsteady on his toes, The Wolf stared into the open casket, and with eyes now wide open, shouted, "Oh m' God. Ish that a diamond in there?"
Twisting around and grabbing Moyshe by the shoulders, he slurred, "Oh m' God. Ish there a diamon' in ever' one of these coffins?"
"Yes, Ivan. And all these caskets are going to be sent to the mayor of Kyiv."
"Why, that greedy bastard," cried The Wolf.
"But Mikhail and I have arranged that all these caskets be delivered to a location of your choosing."
"Ov my choozin? Are you sure? You haf 'ranged all this?"
"Yes. We've been planning this for a long time."
"And every coffin has a diamon' aside?" "See for yourself." Moyshe led The Wolf over to a large single coffin laying just in front of the gangplank to the ship. "Here. Look inside." Still wobbly, The Wolf leaned over the open coffin and stared in.
"I can't shee good. I don't shee a diamond in this one. Light 'nother mash."

As Moyshe put his hand in his pocket, Mikhail came suddenly out from the darkness, and both young men pushed the giant mightily into the open casket. Amidst the screaming, they slammed the lid and battened down the latches. They snapped several locks securely in place. Just then, two burly dock workers lifted the coffin, hefted up the gangplank and into the rusted hold of the ship. With a sudden burst of activity, several sailors began loading and piling the rest of the caskets onto the ship.

"Captain Peter told me that the coffins, none with diamonds, mind you, would be delivered to China in about three or four months. He also wanted to thank you for your generous donation," smiled Mikhail.

He flipped Moyshe's diamond back to him, and the pair walked off to retrieve their wagon filled with the remaining Bessarabian wine.

Chapter 7
Before the Storm

This is the first thing I told myself that I would do, thought Natalya. *I never believed in miracles, but here it is.*

She took the birdcage from its hook and walked outside to the front stoop of her one-room rattrap. She opened the cage door. The two parakeets hesitated, looked at her simultaneously, and swooped out of the cage and up to a nearby rooftop. The green and blue birds waited for a moment, side by side, and then flew out of sight.

Moyshe gave the biggest of his diamonds to Natalya and Anatoly. He asked them to sit on the bed together one morning as he removed the sparkly gem from his pocket.

"For all you have given me, done for me, no questions asked." The graying couple looked at one another, shifted their eyes back and forth, afraid to react, afraid to smile, afraid to say a word. They sat on the edge of their bed for the rest of the day, staring at the enormous, shiny stone. They passed it from one to the other and back again.

How could this be? thought Natalya. *Is he in trouble?*

Are we in trouble? thought Anatoly.

Natalya did not lift a finger to do any washing. Anatoly sat with his eyes wide open, an inextinguishable toothless smile on his old, unshaven, grizzled face. As Natalya gazed at the clear, faceted rock in her hand, her almost-forgotten dreams came rushing in…dreams of a proper house and home, dreams of no longer rubbing her knuckles raw scrubbing other's garments, dreams of clothes and shoes and food on the table at every meal, dreams of her own garden that her Anatoly would tend and a grove of trees that he could cut for firewood to keep them warm in the winter. A chill traversed her shoulders and spread down her spine. *I haven't felt like this in a very long time,* she thought.

***

Moyshe-Yakov Schteinkov moved into the former residence of The Wolf. To the surprise of the arm of the law and the underworld of

Odessa alike, the head of the Jewish Mafia was mysteriously never seen nor heard from again. Within the year, Moyshe had two other housemates: his lovely wife Esther and his healthy and beautiful son Nikolai. He gave the eight black poodles from France to Mikhail who sold each of them for 1000 rubles or more. A clean slate.

No one knew how or from where the name The Fox originated. The partnership of the two hoodlums was well recognized in the four corners of Odessa. The transition of power within the Russian Jewish Mafia of the thriving seaport was seamless. Moyshe, The Fox, became the titular leader of the Odessa Underworld until his death. The Lion Brothers (a name they converted into a legitimate import/export company) understood that any and every crumb of profit, power, successes as well as failures were shared equally. Mikhail bought a fine house on Primorsky Boulevard. He could walk to the Odessa Opera House. He once again resumed his piano instruction with one of the most celebrated piano composers of Ukraine. He was Nikolai's Uncle Mikhail of course, and they discussed much about the piano, music, and the world at large.

"Uncle Mikhail, is it true what they say about my father?"

"Like what? What are you talking about?"

"You know. The stories. The stuff he does."

"I don't know what you're talking about. All I know is that your father is The Fox. And you know what they say, 'Smart as a fox'. That's all you've got to know about your father."

***

Nikolai had the run of the Schteinkov's vast seaside estate. He felt protected and roamed the manicured property overlooking the cliffs bordering the Black Sea. He played in the pine forest at the rear of the house with his Cavalier King Charles Spaniel, Boris. Before the age of five, he was introduced to his first piano teacher, as was the case with every young man in that part of the world whose family could afford a piano or violin tutor. This was the world where pianists, violinists, and composers thrived, lived and breathed, giants who made the world hold their breaths–Vladmir Horowitz, Shuva Cherkassky, Nathan Milstein (born in Odessa), Sergei Prokofiev, and Leo Ornstein, to name a few. The teacher told Moyshe and Esther their son's piano skills were brilliant. All seemed right with the world in the Schteinkov household.

Nikolai, now nine years old, was sent to private school where he thrived. He was tall for his age, with intelligent, hazel eyes, wavy auburn hair, and energy that wouldn't quit. His mother Esther adoringly gave him singing lessons. More to his liking, she hired an art teacher to broaden the horizons of her *boychik*. She carried his easel and canvas to the precipice of the cliffs to banter with him about color, and lighting and brush strokes.

Nikolai looked forward to Grandpa Anatoly coming to help him with his own garden during season…snow peas, string beans, tomatoes, and eggplants with a skirt of blue and pink alyssum. Grandma Natalya visited often, always nicely dressed, smelling of perfume, bearing gifts–books for her grandson. She was healthier and felt younger than ever before, enjoying the best foods from the best markets… smoked salmon, sturgeon, mackerel, sweet beets, the finest sunflower oils, and freshly baked Sharlotka. She would invite him weekly to her beautiful house with chickens and goats in the yard, a beautiful garden, and a surrounding forest of birch, ash, and spruce whose trails he and his grandparents walked. The soothing smell from her new wood-burning stove filled the boy's nostrils, while he spied on Anatoly when he practiced woodworking and cared for the animals in a small adjacent barn. She cooked her grandson his favorite meals such as roasted pig with gravy and spit-fired lamb with mushrooms and baked his best-loved sweets.

***

The year was 1904. Czar Nicholas II had been ruling for ten years. For decades in the Russian Empire, nothing had been stable in the political realm. Over a hundred years ago, the Streltsy revolted, nearly killing Tsar Peter the Great and his half-brother Ivan. In 1881 Tsar Alexander was assassinated by "The People's Will. "Instability, unrest, and killings of civilians reigned, to speak nothing of the Civil War, the

Revolution, and the Red Terror that were soon to rain down on the Russian Empire.

Times were always precarious for certain cultures, particularly the Jews. Thousands were killed in the 1881 pogroms (the Jews were blamed for the assassination of Alexander II). Anytime, anywhere, the Cheka were authorized to attack and did so in smaller versions of well-known nationally-coordinated pogroms. In Odessa, fierce Christian competitors played a role in these pogroms, and as the nineteenth century progressed, the Russian populace became increasingly Antisemitic. In Odessa, Jews were perceived by the general populace as an economic threat. They represented over a third of the population. The Lion Brothers were certainly seen by many as men with power, wealth, influence–as part of the Jewish threat.

The Lion Brothers Import and Export business enjoyed success after success. With the right bit of money laundering and extortion, their business blossomed into an unlimited buying and selling enterprise. Goods ranged from machinery (especially the latest farm equipment), furs, and silk clothing (expanding the silk trade with China), and grain products. Vast quantities of sunflower seeds and sunflower oil came from the rich soil of the Steppes of the Ukrainian river valleys, making Ukraine the world's largest exporter of sunflower oil.

Business exploded. The Lion Brothers continued to expand. They acquired warehouses all over the city. They purchased storage space near the seaport as well as repository facilities on the outskirts of town. They exchanged high-end, more luxurious products, multiple shiploads of goods to and from the five continents.

But the winds of war blew unrest… antisemitism, government authoritarianism, repressive autocracy and resistance to the same. Kernels and embers of The Revolution ignited. The Russo-Japanese War erupted in early 1904. The once thriving commercial centers of Odessa suffered an economic downturn, as did the entire Russian Empire. The rumblings of the Kishinev Pogrom in Bessarabia echoed throughout the city and around the world.

"You're not going to believe it!" screamed Mikhail to Moyshe, as he walked through the door with Kasha the Knife trailing behind.

"That shipment from Coventry, from the Daimler Motor Company, an entire boat filled with Daimler Motor Last Wagons, and engines for boat launches–STOLEN!"

"Whoa, whoa, whoa, my friend. Mikhail, what are you talking about? That shipment was docked several days ago. The shipment was to be unloaded this morning."

"That's what I'm trying to tell you." Mikhail looked nervously at Moyshe and then to Kasha.

"He's right, boss. That son of a bitch English captain. A guy named Elwood Dunn sailed off just after midnight. We paid fifty thousand rubles for that merchandise. Never unloaded the goods. Not sure where he's off to. Some say, Paris."

"Why, that bastard. When I find him, and I will, I'll cut his throat from ear to ear," cried Mikhail.

Moyshe's eyes turned black. His face morphed to purple. He stood speechless. And then his face relaxed. His swarthy complexion returned. He cleared his throat and calmly said to his underling, "Kasha, you will follow this man, Elwood Dunn, to the ends of the earth. You will see where he delivers the goods. You will follow him for weeks, months, if necessary. And we will wait. And wait some more. The three of us will devise a plan."

"What kind of plan? That's a lot of money. After gutting this guy from chin to *pupik*, we're still out fifty thousand rubles," growled Kasha.

"No gutting. You follow him. We are three smart guys. We'll get our revenge. We'll get back our pride and our money."

Chapter 8
Revenge

Though the winter months dragged on, art and music filled Moyshe's home. His growing son was playing the piano with remarkable expertise. He played on several of the renowned stages in Odessa to resounding applause. Both Mikhail and Nikolai studied at the Odessa National Music Academy (where just outside, as a destitute street urchin, Moyshe caught his first pigeon). How could a budding pianist not be inspired by the gold mine of contemporary Russian/Ukrainian classical composers: Balakirev, Mussorsky, Tchaikovsky, Borodin, Rimsky-Korsikov, Rachmaninov, Stravinsky? The house wafted with Nikolai's favorite, Alexander Glazunov's "Seasons." Esther's singing permeated their mansion. And why not? Moyshe's beautiful wife was to give birth to a second child in the spring.

As April rolled into May, business remained good despite growing turmoil–political, ethnic, economic–in Ukraine. The city of Odessa was not immune to the turbulence. As if protected from the black cloud spreading across Tsar Nicholas's domain, the Lion Brothers business prospered, now becoming one of the world's most prosperous exporters of the purest sunflower oil.

"The trap's been set, boss," said Kasha, as he sat around the table drinking vodka with Moyshe and Mikhail at The Fox's home.

"I've been following that prick, Elwood Dunn, around the globe, for months by myself, or through information provided by sea captains, sailors, dock workers, and merchants I know. He did deliver our merchandise, our Daimler trucks and engines, to a company in France. And he got paid for the lot. Again."

"Let's lay out the plan once more," said Moyshe. The three had been working on this strategy for months.

"OK. This asshole has been staying away from Odessa for good reason."

"You bet your ass he has."

"He's been captaining shipments from London to Paris to Constantinople. All over the fucking place. But never here in our fair city, of course."

"So did you catch up with the little shit?"

"You bet we did. Through our contacts, Mikhail and I arranged for a French shipping business to hire this Elwood Dunn to captain a ship, *Le Canard*, to Odessa. An offer the asshole could not refuse."

"No shit. Good going."

"The ship will arrive with 5,000 empty barrels to be filled with the sunflower oil we will sell to them."

"Do they know it's us?"

"Of course not."

"Monsieur Dubois, who represents a very important grain and oil network between France and England, will accompany this bastard to finalize the deal with us. We have four round tanks, each sixty feet in diameter and thirty feet high, filled with our finest sunflower oil in the north end of the city. We will sell these four vats of sunflower oil to this Frenchman, who will sell it to his English buyers in London."

"At what rate?"

"The going rate for this oil, much desired and scarce in England at the moment, is 150,000 rubles, three times the amount that bastard stole from us 3 months ago."

"Go ahead, Kasha, I'm listening," said Moyshe.

"This Frenchman will be untrusting and will want to check our product before filling his barrels with our pure sunflower oil. The captain of the ship will be unaware that we know who is at the helm of the ship."

"I've never met this scoundrel or this Mr. Dubois," said Moyshe.

"And they've never seen you. That's why you'll be showing Mr. Dubois, and hopefully this coward, the vats of sunflower oil and proof of product."

"We have the ladders ready? And the spigots are three feet off the ground?" asked the boss.

"Yes. Yes."

"I know the rest of the plan. You, of course, will be my assistant at all times, Kasha?"

"With pleasure. I can't wait to get my hands on this shithead. The ship will arrive next week, the last week in May." Moyshe filled all three glasses to the brim with his finest vodka.

"*L'chaim,*" they cheered in unison as they clicked glasses and guzzled down their shots.

***

One week later, *Le Canard* sailed into port. Monsieur Dubois and Captain Dunn were escorted by motor car to the outskirts of Odessa, where stood the four enormous oak casks of sunflower oil owned by the Lion Brothers. Moyshe and Kasha were already there and introductions were made.

"I'm sorry but business is business, as they say. For this large of a financial exchange, I must check the tanks to make sure of the product's authenticity," said Dubois.

"Bien sur, monsieur," said Moyshe to the Frenchman, trying to make his buyer as comfortable as possible. "I would do the very same myself. Please come with me."

He handed the two gentlemen a Murano glass goblet and led the way toward the first of four gigantic wooden vats. "As you can see, the tanks all have a spigot. Please feel free to test the contents."

Dubois stepped quickly to the first vat. He perceived the subtle flowery/nutty smell of the oil as he approached. He tried turning the spigot but found it difficult. He finally turned it fully and a clear liquid poured out into his goblet. He dipped his finger, brought it to his lips and tasted.

"Excellent," he said and offered some to the captain. Moyshe and Kasha smiled silently. Dubois shuffled to the second vat and again struggled with the spigot but it finally released the same clear product. Again, he shared this with Dunn.

"Very good," said the captain.

Dubois scooted to the third vat, the other three trailing close behind, and repeated the arduous procedure. The third spigot was hardest yet. Grunting and groaning, he finally said, red-faced, "I may need some help with this one," looking at Kasha. Kasha stepped forward and with a quick and easy flick of his wrist, he opened the spigot and filled the Frenchman's goblet. Same taste-test result.

As he stepped toward the fourth vat, Monsieur Dubois turned with a sheepish grin and said, "Well, just what I hoped for and expected. The product is the purest sunflower oil I have ever sampled. No need to go further. I trust you."

Elwood Dunn leaned over and spoke into monsieur's ear so that all present could hear.

"But sir, with all due respect, how can you be sure that the vats are filled to the top?"

"Aha, I predicted that you might have your doubts. I, myself, would want to be as thorough as possible," said Moyshe quickly, with a smile ear to ear.

"Kasha, would you please fetch the ladder for Monsieur Dubois?"

Kasha ran behind the fourth vat, emerging with a thirty-five -foot ladder that he braced against the fourth vat in just the right spot. It seemed wobbly.

"S'il vous plait," said Kasha. "On the contrary, we insist that you check the level of sunflower oil at the top of the vat."

He looked at Dubois and extended his hand toward the bottom rung of the ladder and swept it in slow motion to the top of the ladder.

A little cross-eyed, Dubois cleared his throat and said, "Since heights are not my forte, I would appreciate the captain doing the sampling on this occasion."

"Certainly," said Elwood Dunn. He boldly began to climb the creaky wooden ladder as he had scrabbled the rat lines on his sailing vessels hundreds of times before.

The captain was a bit unsteady with his glass goblet in one hand. He lost his grip a few times, almost falling. The ladder swayed wildly in the wind. He clenched tighter and steadied his position at the top. Kasha shouted, "You'll find a small door with a latch at the top. Unlatch it and swing it open."

With the long ladder tipping one way and then the other, the captain, sweat pouring off his brow, followed instructions. He tugged open the small door, and dipped his goblet into the pure sunflower oil brimming the vat. Awkwardly, he dipped a thumb into the gleaming liquid and put it to his lips.

"True to your words, sirs. I've not tasted a finer product," the captain shouted.

"It's a bit hard to lock the door again," yelled Kasha, "but you must do so to keep the oil fresh." While Dunn struggled with the difficult lock, straining to balance as the wind picked up, Monsieur Dubois exclaimed,

"Time is of the essence. I'd appreciate transportation back to the ship so we can fill our barrels as soon as possible. We have no trust issues here. We do have deadlines."

"Of course, Monsieur Dubois. An authorized note for 150,000 rubles from you and we'll have an automobile waiting to carry you back to the ship."

"I have already prepared this for you, sir."

He pulled out the note, signed it, and presented it to Moyshe.

"Please," said The Fox as he pointed to Dubois's transportation back to the ship. As the car drove off, Elwood Dunn yelled from above, "I've finally got it. The door is secured."

"Yes. Yes. The door is fine, but I'm afraid you're not," yelled the boss of Lion Brothers Import and Export Company.

"Whatever do you mean?" shouted the captain.

At that point, four of The Fox's strongest men appeared from behind vat number four and lifted the ladder, turned and twisted it in such a way that the poor captain came crashing down to the ground from thirty feet as the ladder followed on top of him. The four men picked up the groaning, moaning, and bruised Elwood Dunn and dragged him off to places unknown. He was never seen or heard from again.

While Dubois's men filled their barrels and loaded them onto the ship, Dubois somehow could not find his captain. He spent days looking for Dunn unsuccessfully. And when they drained all the oil, he was short over five hundred barrels. Suspiciously, most of the oil from vat number four appeared very thin and almost the consistency of water. When an outraged Monsieur Dubois searched Odessa for the Lion Brothers, he was told that if he valued his life, he would end his search immediately. A week went by. No captain. For fear that his product (despite the diminished quantity) would spoil, and fearing for his safety, Dubois found another captain at an outrageous price to sail out of the Odessa seaport.

***

Moyshe and his men sat at the seaport café watching the wake of *Le Canard* move slowly out to sea. Schmuel the Shark, one of those who helped dispose of Captain Elwood Dunn, said, "So, Kasha, let me get this straight. Vat number one, two, and three, all thirty feet tall, had spigots at three feet from the ground. You filled those vats with only four feet of sunflower oil. The rest of those vats were empty. No more oil. When they turned on the spigots for a taste test, sunflower oil poured out. No problem. Vat number four, you filled with water except for the last three feet from the top. You then layered three feet of sunflower oil atop the water. When the captain tested the top of number four, he sampled pure sunflower oil, not knowing that the rest of the vat was filled with water."

"You are correct, my friend," said Kasha. "And God help the French fellow when he arrives in London with a fraction of his sunflower oil order, and receives little to none of his expected payment from an outraged British buyer."

"Yes," said H'avram. "And we screwed both the French and English who helped those fucking Turks stick it to us in our last war in Crimea."

"I'll drink to that," said The Fox, who poured all present another glass of vodka.

"*L'chaim.* To our success."

Just then, Dmitri ran into the café, out of breath.

"Boss. Boss. Come quickly. Your wife is in labor. Esther is with the midwife at your house. The midwife said there may be some trouble."

Chapter 9
The Storm

Since the Battleship Potemkin incident in June 1905, Odessa suffered constant unrest. Skirmishes continued in a staccato fashion throughout the summer...a sailor's revolt, strikes by workers' unions, student and radical uprisings, hundreds killed. The citizenry as well as the authorities blamed it all on the Jews. The Jews were perceived as owning all the factories, all the banks, all the businesses, and all the power, none of which could have been further from the truth. In the late nineteenth century, hundreds of pogroms were happening in small towns and villages across the Russian Empire. Jews, Italians, Greeks, and other foreign nationalities witnessed Odessa as a center of liberal vibe. Its population doubled in size since 1850.

"Foreigners" had always been mistrusted by the Russian people. There was a long- standing prejudice against the Jews in general, (who weren't members of the all-powerful Russian Orthodox Church) in the thriving metropolis of Odessa. Social, political, economic, and religious competition were rife between the Jews and Gentiles. This unstable conflict was not new to Moyshe. He had been there before, as a child. That summer of 1905 he built a ten-foot concrete wall around his estate. His men protected his family atop the wall around the clock. He wasn't taking any chances this time.

But it almost didn't matter anymore. In that first week in June, he raced home from the docks where he had been celebrating with his compatriots over the sunflower oil caper. Reaching home, he heard screaming and yelling coming from the bedroom. Yes, his wife Esther ...his strong, beautiful, talented wife was surrounded by Natalya and what seemed like an army of midwives and helpers for the birth of their second child. Chaos. Screeching. Loud sobbing. Unlike the controlled tension with the birth of his first born.

Suddenly, a frightening silence sunk his heart. A knowingness took hold of him. His insides disappeared. Natalya emerged from the bedroom, drenched in sweat, tears rolling, lips quivering. A frown distorted her face. Moyshe stood, holding his son Nikolai's hand, knowing.

"The baby had the cord around her neck," cried Natalya. "She couldn't breathe. The doctor said your beloved died of heart failure. I thought the shortness of breath, the fatigue, the swelling was normal. Her heart was failing this last month. The stress was too much."

"Papa, where's Momma? Where's the new baby?"

Moyshe-Yakov gripped the boy's hand tightly, turned, and walked out into the yard toward the cliffs, staring at the dark Odessa horizon. Unthinkable. The wound, opened again. Only deeper this time. If that were even possible. And the boy? Dark gray clouds covered the sky as the two trudged down the path to the beach. Nikolai wrenched his hand away and ran and ran and ran until his father caught up to him. His father picked him up and squeezed him in his arms. They both cried and cried together for a long time.

Yet, somehow, tragedy begets tragedy.

***

As dry, brittle kindle is destined to burst into flames at the slightest provocation, the 1905 pogrom began in Odessa. No one was quite clear who the enemy was–the Jews, the Gentiles, the local police, the members of the national army, the radicals, the students? Jewish plots? It was a massacre. Hundreds of Jews were slaughtered. Thousands of Jewish businesses destroyed. The severe antisemitic cruelty drew international attention. The violence, the terror, the shooting and killing and wounding and burying lasted for five days. Local police looked the other way. Then the smoke cleared. All was still.

Unscathed, Moyshe felt things would be safe now. Especially as he had ordered his men to offer a donation to the Cheka, officers and patrolman alike, days before the shooting ignited. Moyshe and his son were protected, as his men stood atop his ten-foot wall. And when Mikhail signaled all clear on the final day of unrest, Moyshe stood at the open door to the mansion. He turned, intending to retrieve Natalya and his only son Nikolai, who were hiding in the tunnel beneath the house that led out to the Black Sea shoreline. An eerie quiet. All the hate and venom had been released. Billowing smoke dissipating into the sky. The metallic smell of blood and throngs of mutilated wounded left in the streets.

With no warning, a split second, a lone gunman snuck through the iron gate and squeezed off three rounds, shooting Moyshe in the back, before Mikhail subdued the murderer of The Fox.

Chapter 10
Survival Redux

"It's getting cold," said Natalya to the boy. "Your grandmother Schteinkov made this coat and hat for your father and you. I had them cleaned, new linings sewn, and torn areas replaced. The fabric is beautiful. They look like new. They are a little bit big now, but nothing that rolling up the sleeves and a bit of stuffing in the hat brim won't fix for the time being. You will grow into them soon. Your mother would be proud of you."

Four diamonds left now, she thought. Two in the hat and two in the coat. She'd use them wisely. That she promised herself.

She was afraid of Nikolai wandering outside the picket fence that surrounded her small home. She was not young any more, but not so old either. What choice did she have? She'd done it once before, and she'd do it again. Strong. Ukrainian strong. During the October unrest, she hung the Russian Orthodox or Suppedaneum Cross on the gate. Her house was one of the few in the neighborhood not burned to the ground. Perhaps things were no different now in 1905 as they were during the previous pogroms in Odessa that took place in 1821, 1859, 1871, and 1891...anti-Jewish hatred, killing, maiming, burning.

Nikolai took piano lessons at home now but his effort was lackluster. Over and over his playing devolved into a joyless rendition of Glazonov's "Seasons" and nothing else. He walked limply and stared through people, the piano keys, the food placed in front of him. When pushed to continue his painting, he avoided the seascapes, landscapes, and forest scenes. He replaced those scenes now with canvas after canvas, showing dark, multicolored blotches of nothingness.

"Speak to me, *Bubala.* You don't talk to me anymore," Natalya pleaded with a forced grin, looking down at her grandson's sad eyes. She tried to imagine what was inside that young head: sadness, loneliness, fright, disorientation, hopelessness, helplessness, anger, anxiety? Lost. Perhaps the way some people with Alzheimer's might feel? But at 10 years old? Yes, it was all of the above but it was mostly the missing of it all: the missing of his mother's kind eyes, her loving smile, her warm hugs, his father's laugh, his intelligent eyes, the strong hand that would hold his when they walked. The blank stares broke her heart, the same way her heart ached thirty years ago.

***

Nikolai spent his time reading in his new room at Natalya's house. The house was lonely, not as he remembered it when he used to visit. Especially now that Grandpa Anatoly had died. Consumption. He was buried behind the synagogue in the Moldavanka neighborhood. Natalya would have the boy help her in the kitchen making thumb cookies, his favorite small round shortbread cookies with a shallow thumbprint in the center filled with strawberry jam. He sat quietly at the kitchen table eating his share while his Grandma drank her coffee Russian style–holding the sugar cube between her front teeth, sipping her coffee loudly as it permeated the cube turning it brown, trickling into her mouth to inspire a smile.

Natalya was quieter now–absent minded, less outgoing. She often stopped mid-sentence and thought of that awful scene, with Esther breathless, the purple baby, and the young mother directing her to fetch the letter from the bedside table. Natalya read it a thousand times in the weeks following Esther's demise, and another thousand times after the death of her husband, Moyshe.

My Dear Esther

These are troubled times. Please promise that if my life were to come to an end, you will take our remaining family to America. In honor of my mother's wishes, Nikolai will soon fit into the hat and coat that has been passed to him. I am sure these garments will help you in times of need.

Know that I love you always,
Moyshe-Yakov Schteinkov

***

Four diamonds left. Of course, one had been given to Mikhail, Moyshe's Lion Brother to the end. Natalya knew they had to move. Move far away. Her beloved Anatoly may not have agreed. To a foreign place? When millions, some said 3 million, Russians were emigrating to America? And who did she know? What was there? Foreigners with strange ways. And with her prized possession in tow? She didn't know the language. But he did. He was tutored for years and was now fluent in that strange English tongue. He read exclusively about this strange land and, if he talked at all, would tell her about the tall buildings, the rich people, about New York City, Chicago, New Orleans and Boston.

Now the ten-year-old avoided talk with his Uncle Mikhail about world-renown composers or famous countrymen as his heroes. He would excitedly talk about the new music, Jazz…a rising tide of melodies, impromptu phrases, improvisations, and creative cadences. These sounds were reaching across the ocean played by names like Jelly Roll Morton, James P. Johnson, and others (Fats Waller, Art Tatum, Duke Ellington) soon to rise. Nikolai now heard rumors about other new heroes in the big, shining cities of America like Lucky Luciano, Bugsy Siegel, and an up-and-coming Chicago star, Alphonse Capone.

His frustrated art teachers stopped trying to teach him about the light from the North during the day that was the most stable and reliable for his painting. He no longer cared. He inhaled the stories of The Fox, his beloved father whose glorious reputation grew larger as time went on.

***

They planned the trip meticulously. After all, it was illegal to leave Russia–not only for military-aged men, but especially for Jews. The famine was closing in, instability in the Balkans was worsening, hostile alliances formed in the Ottoman Empire, Germany, and Austro-Hungary. Strikes and riots ignited all over the Russian Empire. Opponents challenged Nicholas II's autocracy from every direction.

They set up networks and arranged travel with professional smugglers, paid bribes delicately. They arranged food, tickets, and accommodations. And above all, they maintained secrecy.

"Wake up, Nikolai. Wake up. We have to go," whispered Natalya.

"Now? Where? In the middle of the night?" Nikolai said, with one eye open in the dark.

"Yes. Get dressed and come downstairs now. Mikhail is waiting."

Nikolai rubbed his eyes, dressed, and ran to Uncle Mikhail at the front door.

"Nikolai, my *banditýl*, we have to go."

"But where? Where are we going?" said the boy looking up, clearly ready to go to the ends of the earth with his father's comrade.

"It is a secret but I will tell you. Only if you can keep a secret and tell no one. Can you?"

"Yes. Yes. I will tell no one!"

Mikhail bent down and whispered in the boy's ear, "You are going to America. Shhh. You must do what Natalya and I say." The boy's eyes grew wider, his eyebrows reached for his widow's peak, and the huge "O" that his mouth formed could have let in ten flies. A big smile flashed across his face, his heart was thumping in his chest. *A dream come true?* Thought Nickolai. *Was he really going to* America, *the land of New Orleans, Buddy Bolden, and Tommy guns?*

As he rushed Nikolai and Natalya outside toward the front of the house, Mikhail said softly, "Now you and grandma climb up into the wagon and lie down under the tarpaulin. The journey is long."

PART II

Chapter 11
America

Mikhail and the wagon driver rolled through the night via Kirshinev and on toward the Moldova border. At the border, Mikhail jumped down from the wagon, lifted the corner of the tarp, squeezed Natalya's hand, hugged the sleeping boy, and disappeared into the darkness. Within another twenty-four hours, the precious cargo arrived at the train station in Chivinau.

"Grandma, where are we? Are we in *you-know-where*?"

"No, Niki. We have a very long passage before we reach *you-know-where.*"

She and the boy climbed stiffly out of the wagon and sorted tickets for the train…many tickets.

"These tickets will take you to Belgrade, then Budapest, Vienna, Prague, Hanover and finally to Hamburg. From there, you will board a ship for America," said the driver. "*Oodachi.*"

She grabbed her bag, took Nikolai's hand, and they stepped onto the train. They took their seats as the whistle blew.

"You look handsome in your father's hat and coat," Natalya leaned over and whispered in Nikolai's ear.

***

"Your seascape looking over the cliffs, the beach, the ocean is coming along nicely, Nikolai."

"But Momma, what's beyond the horizon? What's out there? Will we ever go there?"

"Nikolai, not all that's out there is always so nice. I hope you don't experience the darkness for a long time," his mother said as she walked back to the house. Nikolai thought for a bit, and painted a blackbird, indistinct, in the distant sky. Then another, and another, and another until he filled the canvas with blackbirds, obfuscating the art beneath. The blackbirds flew out of the picture and swirled around the boy. They squealed and squawked and buzzed around his head. They circled closer

and closer, hundreds of them. They pecked at him. He was helpless. He tried protecting himself but the birds followed him wherever he ran. He started screaming as loud as he could and....

Nikolai woke in a sweat. He sat up in the creaky bed. His heart was pounding. He didn't recognize his surroundings at first. Where was he? A shabby room, paint peeling off the walls, Natalya standing over a pot atop a tiny oven.

"Grandma?" asked Nikolai.

Natalya looked over her shoulder, "Yes, I know. New surroundings, a new world, not so nice. Believe me, I know. Are you OK? You had another bad dream."

"Grandma, tell me again what happened on our trip to America," his two fists twisting in his eye sockets to further expel the frightening nightmare.

His brain was as active and bright as it would ever be. It would take some time for his physicality and true grit to catch up. What happens to a soul, a field productive with wild flowers and fruit trees and grains, growing to the sky, and tall green forests bordering this lush fertile land, when a weapon of mass destruction suddenly annihilates this bucolic landscape?

"Oy, yoy, yoy. I have told you a hundred times."

"Please, just one more time."

"We were lucky. We could have been killed or raped or left by the side of the road. But your Uncle Mikhail arranged everything. I don't know how he did it. Down to Green Eyes meeting us at the boat. It was 1907," said Natalya, a cigarette hanging from the right side of her mouth as she bent over the stove. She was making a batch of rugelach--a bite-sized pastry of rolled flakey dough, butter, nuts, sugar, cinnamon, and strawberry jam--Nikolai's favorite. The cigarette ash grew longer and longer, curling downward until *puff*, the gray column fell into the mixing bowl and blended with the batter. She sat down at the kitchen table, joints aching and groaned, "Stinking habit. I never smoked these filthy things until I got to America."

She grabbed a sugar cube from the sugar bowl, placed it between her front teeth and siphoned a mouthful of the bitter coffee. She let out a big sigh.

"It was a long journey. Trucks, and horse-drawn wagons, and trains, and boats. We walked sometimes. Night and day. The trains were crowded. Butt to butt. Most had to stand. The orthodox Jews sat on water bottles, especially on Sabbath… I think because it was OK to travel by boat on Shabat but not by train. It was cold, and we only had one blanket between us. You were good. You hardly made a peep. In fact, I don't know if you even talked the whole time. We slept mostly on the trains, in the stations, in the wagons, but once or twice we stayed at inns. Or really the homes of widows, mostly Jewish. Sort of an underground railroad. We put the money owed, as we left, on the corner of the table under the table cloth …I think maybe because if it was the Sabbath, they weren't supposed to take money on that day. And food. Food was a problem. Some days, some bread but usually just potatoes. Oy vey, I never want to see another potato in my life."

"And the ship. It was winter, December, and the seas were rough. We tossed and heaved and everybody was sick. Any food we had, slid right off the table. But we were fortunate, again, because of your Uncle Mikhail. We got to sleep in a bunk, you and I together on a bottom bunk, all crammed in. An *alta cocker*, this grubby old man, sleeping above us snored so loud, I think he woke God. And every time he snored, you'd jump up and twist his big toe hanging off the upper bunk as hard as you could, and he'd stop snoring for a while. It was an old military boat, and it stunk…sweat and mold and oily. It was crowded, and noisy, and God forbid if you had to pish."

"Were we excited about coming to America?"

"Excited? We were scared to death. Terrified. What did you know? You were too little to understand what was going on. And I was too old. We had no idea where we were going except *to America.* Who would be there when we arrived? Where would we go? An old lady and her grandson–who knew what to do? A million things could have gone wrong, and almost did but Mikhail planned and paid for our tickets, and bribes, and tips and places to sleep. Almost one month it took to get across to Hamburg. Until we got on that ship."

"Was it the Red Star?"

"Yes," said Natalya. "But we almost boarded the wrong ship. We were in line and about to go onto the boat to America when suddenly a bunch of policemen pushed a dozen of us into a different line. That line was going to Palestine."

"So what happened then, Grandma?"

"You know perfectly well what happened then. I have told you this story a million times."

"Tell me one more time," Nikolai said to Natalya with that puppy-dog look which he knew and she knew she couldn't resist.

"Well, at the last minute, this older, but tall and handsome man, with bright emerald green eyes, grabbed my arm and held your hand tight and pulled us back in the line for the boat to America."

"And we arrived in Boston?"

"Yes. Well, they sent a certain number of Jews to Massachusetts, a certain number to Rhode Island, some to Baltimore, and a certain number to New York. We stood in line at the immigration center at the wharf in Boston and they asked us our name and I didn't want to get separated from you, so I said both our names were Schteinkov after your parents. But the immigration officer kept stumbling over our name until finally the man with the green eyes who stood in back of us shouted out, 'Stein, Stein'. So they put down Stein, and that became our name. This man, he told the officers, his name was Stein as well. I don't remember exactly how we got to East Boston, to this place on Gove Street, down the block from the synagogue."

"But you forgot to tell the part about Mr. Shapiro."

"Oh, yes. So we were standing in line and the official asked, 'And who is your contact?' I didn't understand the language, never mind know what to say."

"You can't be released if you have no sponsor, no address to live," he said. "You and your boy will have to go to the settlement house, maybe North End Union. You get in line over there."

The official was about to slam down his inked rubber stamp when the man with green eyes said, “No, no, wait, wait. They are with me. We live at 324 Gove Street. Let’s go home, right now.”

“I must have nodded in agreement. Green Eyes, Mr. Shapiro, took my arm, grabbed hold of your hand, grabbed my suitcase with the other hand and we walked outside into the sunshine.”

Three diamonds left, thought Natalya. The money had been well spent. Mikhail had arranged every step of the way. Harold Shapiro settled them in a third-floor-walkup, two rooms, bathroom down the hall. Welcome to America.

Chapter 12
Boston

"Watch out!" someone yelled. Nikolai jumped back just in time to keep from being hit by the trolley. The fourteen-year-old young son of The Fox wasn't in Odessa anymore. Below his third-floor window in East Boston, he heard the ear-splitting sound of the trolleys trundling down the tracks, the loud, incessant bells and whistles, honks of scattered automobiles, and the shouts of peddlers calling out in English, German, Russian, Yiddish and Hebrew. They echoed from one end of Gove Street to the other. The millions of Eastern European and Russian Jewish immigrants who came to the United States during the first decade of twentieth century made the streets of East Boston noisy and busy and bustling.

The grocer came by in his truck two times a week; the butcher stopped once a week; and the fishmonger visited three times a week with affordable codfish from the Grand Banks. The baker came every day with his black rye and challah. It was his strudel and sponge cake and mandel bread that made Nikolai's eyes pop wide and his mouth water. None of the newcomers could afford the quantity or the quality of the items that their stomachs growled for.

Ohel Jacob, the oldest and largest synagogue located a block away, on the corner of Paris and Gove Streets, was the soul of Jewish culture, education…of life itself in the new world. Natalya, in her late fifties, and Harold Shapiro, a decade younger, attended English language classes at night there.

"Why don't you come with us to *schul*," Natalya pleaded with Nikolai. "You might find comfort in prayer, or maybe meet some people you'd like."

"I have no use for a *house of god*," Nikolai snapped in a defiant tone. Still, he noticed the upright piano standing at the foot of the bimah when Natalya dragged him there from time to time.

***

"Nikolai, are you going to work with Harold today?"

"Yes, he is picking me up this morning."

About a month ago, ever since Nikolai learned Harold's true identity, he began working with Harold after school and on weekends.

"Are you telling the truth, Grandma?" asked Nikolai wide-eyed.

"On my husband's grave. Of course, I am. Remember Uncle Mikhail told you that he lost his parents at a young age and was taken in by his aunt?"

"Yes, I met his Aunt Sasha once or twice at holidays," said Nikolai.

"And do you happen to remember her eyes?"

"Her eyes? Yes. Yes, I do. They were bright, sparkling, green."

"Yes. Emerald green. Just like Mr. Shapiro's eyes. Harold Shapiro is the brother of Mikhail's Aunt Sasha. Mikhail arranged that he look out for us when we arrived in Boston."

Harold started out as a peddler soon after he arrived in Boston. He knew only Yiddish and Russian. He began with only a push-cart. He borrowed the money for the cart, and soon borrowed again to purchase a horse. He peddled dry goods…writing paper, envelopes, pots and pans, fly paper (there were no screens then), needles and thread…anything he could get his hands on to make a profit. He started out in Boston City proper, yet the competition was staggering. He shifted to Sommerville, Cambridge, Dorchester, and Chelsea. Others had survived similarly until they could afford their own shop. No matter how much money Harold earned, it was never enough. Harold took in Nikolai and taught him the trade. Nikolai noticed that there was no job too small for Harold. Harold never "left a dime on the table."

The young wage earner gave most of the money he made to Grandma Natalya. The first thing he bought with the fraction of earnings that he saved for himself was a phonograph. Invented in 1877, Edison's phonograph progressively surged in popularity. The "dog and phonograph" logo of the Victor Talking Machine Company seemed to be in every magazine and newspaper. Jazz played a large part in this phonographic surge. Jazz recordings produced on 78 RPM records were distributed faster than they could be pressed. This accessibility meant that one could listen to Fats Waller's "Honey Suckle Rose" and "Ain't

Misbehavin'," or Hoagy Carmichael's and Mitchell Parish's "Stardust" without leaving the kitchen or living room. Nikolai listened to these recordings over and over.

"That noise. What is that noise?" yelled Natalya. "Are you trying to make me go deaf sooner than I already am? You spend your precious money on this *hazzarai,* this junk?"

"The price of a Victrola has dropped down to fifteen dollars, Grandma."

As time went on, as he grew older and bolder, he'd sneak into nightclubs and other venues hosting this burgeoning new "Devil's music." The sounds swarmed his brain. The musical freedom of this new genre exploded within him. The new Boston subway system could take him to The Harmony Shop, or impromptu "house hops" in Roxbury or to the South End to hear some of the greats. The young baritone saxophonist Harry Carney, alto-saxophonist Johnny Hodges, and tenor saxophonist Paul Gonsalves, were all born, trained and emerged from the Boston area to eventually become the backbone of arguably the greatest jazz band of all time: The Duke Ellington Orchestra.

***

"How was math class today?" asked Natalya when Nikolai returned home one spring evening. Now Nikolai was smart enough to know that Natalya rarely asked him about math class.

"I didn't go to school today."

"Yes, I know because I received a note from your teacher that you have only been to school twice this month."

Nikolai was now working full time with Harold Shapiro. He thought it odd that Harold routinely stopped at various shops along the way, often making no attempt to sell his wares. One warm summer day his mentor weaved through the crowded Boston business district. He stopped abruptly in front of Arnold the Tailor's on Weybosset Street. Harold scooted into the shop. He soon came out and jumped back into the wagon, cracking the reins. As they drove on, Nikolai asked,

"What is that paper bag that you just stuck in your back pocket, Harold?"

"What bag? There's no bag," growled Harold, holding his hand next to the back pocket.

"The bag in your pants that you're trying to hide from me."

"That is nothing of your concern," said Harold sternly. Eyes front, they rode in silencc.

Chapter 13
Heaven

Crash! As they drove their weekly route down Weybosset Street, they both looked quickly to the right. "Holy shit," they said in unison. On the sidewalk in front of Hyman's Music Store ("Pianos and Organs for Sale"), was a mahogany grand piano smashed to pieces. The four legs had broken off and scattered in all directions; one leg was splintered and lying in the middle of the street. The lid was cracked in half and lay askew, and the hardwood rim was dented. People gathered around, oohing. Hyman Rosenberg rushed breathlessly out of his store to assess the damage. A glance upward revealed a ten-foot solid iron hoist with an industrial-sized pulley system of thick ropes cantilevered from a triple wide second-story window facing the street below. A thick rope hung from the second-floor pulley with a frayed, broken end. The remnants of the remaining rope were coiled up on the sidewalk with its own shredded end.

Harold and Nikolai jumped out of the wagon and ran over to the fallen, splintered piano, while Rosenberg stood over the once magnificent instrument, looking up at the broken rope. He had both hands on his head, feigning to pull out the remaining white and grey curly hair that rimmed his baldness.

Miraculously, it appeared that the bruised case contained an intact sound board, treble and base strings, tuning pins, hammers and cast -iron plate. The keyboard and action appeared to be unscathed as well. Harold stood amidst the gawking crowd and said, "What a terrible mess to happen on such a beautiful summer day."

Nikolai stood alongside Harold and stared intently at the musical mess. He knelt in front of the keyboard and fingered the keys. His fingers moved from one end of the keyboard to the other, first playing the twelve major scales and then gliding through the twelve minor scales. People gathered. As Hyman Rosenberg admonished Nikolai for touching his destroyed piano, the crowd protested. One voice shouted at the owner, "Let the boy play."

Nikolai stopped moving his hands for a moment, stretched his fingers, closed his eyes, and played Rachmaninoff's Piano Concerto No.2 in C minor. The crowd hushed. More people crowded around. No one made a sound. It seemed as if neither the sun, the clouds, or the street cars moved. A faint smile peeked out from under Rosenberg's mustache. And then Nikolai's fingers stopped, just for a few seconds. They activated again. Out of the piano's inner workings came a beat, a complex harmony and rhythm. The crowd swayed from one foot to the other, feet tapping. Onlookers exclaimed, "Oh yeah" and "That's it" and "Alright." Nikolai shifted from playing "Black Bottom Stomp", to "Dead Man Blues," and "Turtle Twist". The crowd grew.

"That kid's amazing," someone shouted.

Nikolai's head was in the clouds. He frankly did not know what came over him. This broken instrument with its shiny black casing sang as its gold painted Steinway and Sons reflected the sun on that beautiful summer afternoon. He couldn't stop playing. He felt his body and soul move to the tunes of Jelly Roll Morton's "Kansas City Stomp" and "Wolverine Blues"; songs by James P. Johnson like "Harlem Woogie," "Back Water Blues," and "Sweet Lorraine." The working men and homemakers shifted their hips and tilted their shoulders from side to side.

Harold stood still on the sidewalk of Weybosset Street in the back of that crowd on that sunny afternoon. How, just how, had Nikolai learned to play this jazz, this unconventional music, that broke all the rules, that bubbled up from the Black and Creole community? Certainly not from the East End of Boston with Eastern Asians and Jewish immigrants garbed in prayer shawls and yamakas.

"You were late coming home again last night," said Natalya at breakfast. "Every night now. Where were you?"

"Nowhere, Grandma," he said, hoping no one had seen him coming and going to the synagogue on Gove Street at night. Many months ago, he had been sitting at the piano, trying to play the songs he heard on his phonograph, beating out the rhythm and blues he loved.

"Hey, what are you doing in here? You're not supposed to be in here," said the man in a grey sweatshirt and overalls, leaning on his broom, refraining from sweeping the floor while he stood and listened.

"Why not? I thought God welcomed all His sheep to His house. Besides, the Rabbi says that all are welcome at any time. He said his door is always open."

"Well, we'll see about that." And the janitor wheeled around and walked away. Nikolai pounded away at the piano.

The next night the Rabbi emerged from the darkness of the nave.

"Vos y dos? What is this?" said the Rabbi, looking Nikolai up and down.

Nikolai raised his hands off the keys, raised his head up and looked the Rabbi straight in the eye.

"It's Jazz. A new age. A new sound. I think God would like to hear something new."

The Rabbi had been standing in the shadows listening to this noise. And why shouldn't one of God's creatures, this young Ukrainian immigrant be allowed to express himself? This was the new world. He had recently been trying to open his mind. Perhaps he (and maybe God) would actually come to enjoy this raw, energetic, soulful music as opposed to the maudlin, often morose organ music traditionally played for centuries as part of the Judaic tradition.

The Rabbi looked at Nikolai, grinned beneath his massive mustache and waist-long beard and said, "Hmmm," as he spun around and walked out of the synagogue.

After an hour and a half, Nikolai finished playing and the large crowd began to disperse, but not until they showed their appreciation with an uproarious ovation. Hyman Rosenberg stepped up and looked down at the boy on his knees in front of the keyboard.

"Son, what is your name?"

"Nikolai Stein, sir," said the dark-haired, blue-eyed street boy.

"I see that you can play this stuff," said the piano store owner, scrunching his nose and squinting his eyes like he was seeing and smelling a rotten piece of meat, making his wire-rimmed glasses rise above his eyebrows, "But can you play my stuff…Mozart, Schubert, Chopin?

"Oh, yes, sir," and Nikolai played Debussy's Clair de Lune as sweetly as Hyman had ever heard it played. Hyman Rosenberg's eyebrows came together and his brow wrinkles bulged as he rubbed his chin.

"Young man, would you come work for me in my store?"

Nikolai thought to himself. He was just getting the hang of working with Harold. In fact, Harold, knowing that Nikolai was no longer pursuing his formal education, had recently talked about Nikolai sharing in the business with him, a partner of sorts.

"Well, sir, I already have a job. But what's your job?"

Nikolai imagined himself taking orders from this curmudgeon, being told to move this piano and that organ, polish this baby-grand and that upright.

"I want you to simply play the piano in my shop."

"You want me to play your beautiful Steinways, Bosendorfers, and Bechsteins and that's it?"

"That's it."

"And you'll pay me for this?"

"Yes."

I can't believe it, thought Nikolai. *A job made in heaven.*

Chapter 14
Something's Going On

Nikolai came each day to play at Hyman's Music Store. Heaven. That's what it felt like. Of course, they negotiated the music selection and work hours.

"Nikolai, during peak hours, you must play my choices," Rosenberg said. "Beethoven, Brahms, Mozart, Dvorak."

"And during off hours, I can practice my stuff... 'I've Got Rhythm,' 'Tiger Rag,' and 'Stomping at the Savoy.'"

What a brilliant idea. Nationwide, as the sales of phonographs grew, the sales of pianos sagged. *How sweet is this,* thought Hyman. *Since this musical genius started playing in my store, business is booming. The number one rule in retail: Get them in the door, the rest will take care of itself.* They came in droves from all ends of Boston...passersby, musical enthusiasts, wealthy homeowners, musical directors, and church choir leaders. They came to hear the music, to touch and admire the beautiful instruments, and maybe, just maybe, to buy a new piano or organ for their home, or school, or church, or speakeasy. Rosenberg smiled a lot. Nikolai still couldn't believe it. *I'm living the dream,* he thought.

Harold encouraged Nikolai in his new pursuits and in fact often insisted Nikolai work at Hyman's on Tuesdays and Thursdays, as these were the days he had long, out of town routes and he preferred to be alone.

"Wow, Harold, nice new shiny truck. Business must be good," said Nikolai as he jumped into the vehicle one day.

"Yup," said Harold in a manner that was almost too nonchalant.

"Good for you. You must be proud of yourself."

Harold came to see Nikolai play, once a week. While he listened to the melodies, he walked the floor from piano to piano wiping his hands over the ebony and mahogany lids. He would, it seemed, always take the time to go in the back and talk with Rosenberg. Nikolai, at first, did not notice the bulge in Harold's coat pocket as he would leave the store, wave, and oppose his right-hand thumb and forefinger in an "OK, good job" gesture. Neither did Nikolai seem to notice at first the boss's reddened, scowled face, and tight body language as he emerged from the back following each visit from Harold.

Chapter 15
The Truth Comes Out

They sat in the truck in silence.

"So, Harold," Nikolai said.

"Uh-huh."

"I came into Mr. Rosenberg's store last week. I sat down to play as usual, Mahler's Symphony No. 7, when Mr. Rosenberg strolled by in a casual fashion. Absentminded. It seemed that he didn't want to address me as he usually does. No *Hello.* No *Good morning.* It just seemed like he didn't want to look at me."

"Uh-huh. So?" Harold shifted awkwardly in his seat behind the wheel.

"Well, when he turned to go back to the office, I saw a bruise on his face. A black eye on the left. A big shiner. I stopped playing and walked over to Hyman. I grabbed his arm and asked him what happened. He was fidgety and looked down at the floor. He said, 'Oh, nothing. Nothing…ask your friend Harold.'"

"Uh-huh. So?"

"So, I'm asking you. What happened to Mr. Rosenberg's face?"

Silence.

Harold's face turned red. Nikolai's ears twitched back, his eyebrows rose and his eyes opened wide.

"Harold, I don't know if you've noticed, but I'm going to be 16. Not a kid anymore. And again, I don't know if you've noticed as well, but I'm not stupid."

Silence. "Well, if you're an adult now, and you're so smart, then you know when to keep your mouth shut. It's none of your damn business."

"Yeah, well, how 'bout I make it my business and tell Natalya, and the Rabbi, maybe the police."

"What? What do you know? What would you tell anybody?"

"Well, let's try that you come into Mr. Rosenberg's store every month. You go to the back office and come out with a stuffed envelope that you stick into the inside pocket of your jacket. And he comes out of his office a little while later, swearing like he wants to kill you and your kind. And that you seem to make similar stops at various establishments each week, despite the fact that you don't carry any goods into those places. And that you suddenly have a new truck and new clothes and that fancy new apartment. Not from the money you make selling this shit," said Nikolai, pointing with his thumb to the back of the truck. "How 'bout I tell them that."

Harold blew out a long sigh. He parked the truck. Beads of sweat popped on his brow.

"Look, kid, I'm sorry about your friend Hyman. I got a little too rough with him the other day. Truth is, you're right. You're growing up. And there's stuff you'll find out sooner or later." Harold took a deep breath and let it out noisily.

"You ever hear of Charles Solomon?"

"Just some gossip. People say he's a wiseguy."

"He's more than that. People call him The King. He's from the old country. Like us. He and his brothers are involved here in Boston. Really involved...prostitution, fencing, bail bonding, extortion, some gambling and narcotics. They got guys. Me, I'm a peon. He throws me and some other Jews a bone sometime. Look. You come over here. You don't know the language. You got no money. What was I supposed to do? All of us. In the land of milk and honey. I want some of the honey."

"So you work with prostitutes?"

"No, never. That ain't for me. Me, I collect money."

"You mean you extort money, like from Hyman Rosenberg?"

"Yeah."

"And if he doesn't pay?"

"Well...you saw what happened to that busted up Steinway that you played on the sidewalk?"

"That was you? You destroyed Mr. Rosenberg's piano?"

"Hey, the man's got to pay. For protection."

Silence. The wheels were turning.

"What? A person has to make a buck around here," whined Harold.

Nikolai had never seen this side of Harold. His stomach was in a knot. His chest felt tight. He felt heat surging from his lower spine, up his back, passing through his neck, and exploding in his head. He suddenly turned to Green Eyes. His lips formed the words, uncontrollably,

"Look. I'm warning you Harold. You leave Rosenberg alone. No more. I don't care whatever the fuck else you do. But I'm telling you to lay off Hyman."

Harold's head snapped back, just for a second. Green Eyes quickly recovered, and with eyelids at half-mast, a smirk on his face, said, "Or else what? What are you going to do? Shoot me?"

Nikolai stared at Harold through slits between his eyelids. Dead silence. Nikolai's body…no, his brain was on fire. He opened the door, got out of the truck, and before slamming the door, looked straight into Harold's eyes and said almost under his breath, "Maybe I will."

Chapter 16
Nikolai Emerges

The caterpillar is a beautiful specimen…its colors, the way it moves, a slow majestic travelog. But there are stages. And at just the right time, it constructs its cocoon. The mysterious chrysalis hangs on a limb until just the right moment when it emerges with its DNA giving the Monarch butterfly its glorious paisley colors and patterns. The same DNA that gives this majestic organism its ability to fly, to gather food, to mate, to pollinate and eventually to fly to its imprinted, its designated in-born destination in the hills of the Oyamel Fir Forest along the eastern peninsula of the Mexican State of Michoacaán, to die a frozen death, maybe, maybe not mourned by those left behind.

Through an intricate system of genes, humans pass down from generation to generation traits and talents, human proclivities toward math, or science, or music, or athleticism, or aggressiveness, or introversion, or leadership. And whether it is DNA, or the second by second trappings of our milieu, our environment, that is responsible for "us," has never been clear. These callings seem to pull us with a force greater than the mythological Sirens who drew sailors toward their destinations (and often to their destruction) with their enchanted, irresistible singing.

And so it was that Nikolai was the son of The Fox, a boy-man with talents and abilities cast into an environment where he had no money, no contacts, but dreams of his own and a heritage of The Lion Brothers. He was born in a far-off place where overcrowding, poverty, political and religious conflicts gave birth to a breed toward which Nicholai was drawn.

***

"So what is this I hear? Are you in trouble? I hear bits and pieces? Are you working for that hoodlum Solomon? Huh? King Solomon. King shming. He's dangerous. What about the job you have with that nice Mr. Rosenberg?" Natalya turned her head and made a spitting sound.

"And you better keep your eyes open," she said, knowing her grandson was barely paying attention to her.

"What do you mean, *keep my eyes open*?"

"I've been hearing some things, certain things. Some people aren't always who you think they are."

"Like who, grandma? Who are you talking about?"

"I'm not saying. But Old Green Eyes may not be everything you think he is. You just keep your own eyes open."

"Grandma, Charlie Solomon has money. He can buy things, go places, get out of this East Boston ghetto when he wants. And here we are in this two-room sweaty three-story walk-up. You know as well as I do, we came right after the Russian Revolt of 1905. The old country is splintering and the real revolution is coming. All of Europe is on fire with a world war raging. But there's a musical revolution in the States. Jazz. And it's just starting and I'm going to grab onto that train. And yes, you've heard about King Solomon along with other Jews whose families came from the old country like Harry 'Gyp the Blood' Horowitz and his Lenox Avenue Gang, and Arnold Rothstein in New York City, and Meyer Lansky in Miami, Bugsy Siegel in Las Vegas, the Cohen Brothers in Los Angeles, and Abe Bernstein with his Purple Gang in Detroit. It's in all the newspapers. Their stories are all over the newsreels."

Money was to be had in all types of racketeering, and Nikolai wanted in. He could feel it. He could taste it.

***

Some say that there are genes we can inherit for all types of skills (mechanical, athletic, etc.) and emotions (anger, depression, aggression, etc.) and talents (artistic, musical, etc.) but could this hold true for the heredity of the mobster? Is there a tendency at birth to be a maverick, a person motivated by his want to be a thug, a want for some type of power, an urge to follow in the footsteps of those who want something for nothing? Where does this wish come from…a wish to be oriented toward the need to acquire what that other guy has, but via a different, an alternative route? Perhaps there is a drive toward a faster track, with conscience suspended on the basis of some wrong or tragedy that befell that dark soul in his youth…death/abandonment/poverty/brutality?

Chapter 17
A Lucky Break

The job started off pretty simple. In time, it became very complicated. Though Nikolai's trust in Green Eyes had diminished considerably, it was Harold who got him the gig.

"Hey, kid, I heard they need a piano player at Sharky's."

"Oh yeah."

"The usual piano player quit, or got sick or something. Maybe the flu. I heard from a friend of a friend. King Solomon wants someone immediately. He just bought the old joint at Crosstown, the intersection of Massachusetts and Columbus avenues."

"There's a train that stops near there, isn't there?"

"Yeah. That's the one. He already took down the old sign and put up a new one. Cocoanut Grove or something. Plans to fix it up, make it nice, bigger. It ain't the fanciest joint in town. There are still lots of poor immigrants and a big black population there, but this place is on the border of an up-and-coming neighborhood with nouveau-riche immigrants who seem to be moving on up."

"Ever been there?"

"I was there once, and the crowd is what I'd call mixed."

"Oh yeah. How much are they paying?"

"I don't know what the pay is," said Harold. "But ya' know, you come over here, you have no money, no family, no trade, no job. What the hell are you supposed to do? Sweep the streets? Not me. I'm going to jump on the chance when I see it. Make a buck or two. Maybe more. It's every man for himself in this land of opportunity, kid. Seeing how you're growing up and all, I think you can handle this job. It'll get your foot in the door. So maybe you do a few favors for Mr. Solomon on the side. But I wouldn't tell your grandmother. By the way, I haven't seen her lately. How's she doing?"

***

The new century brought millions of "new Americans" from abroad, all vying for the same niche, any niche. New inventions, a faster world, a shrinking world, filled with suffragettes, and Klansmen, and politicians. Joining the war in Europe was fast becoming more of a reality. The Boston Brahmins continued to wage their fierce battles with the new immigrants.

The latter forces were taking their toll on Natalya. She had not escaped the vicissitudes of immigrant life in America. They had difficult times in Odessa, save for a brief respite. Her experiences in America had not been ideal. *I am old now, she thought. And in my old age, who do I have? Our Mr. Green Eyes now seems to be more interested in Mr. Solomon and his gangster cronies, than in helping to support us. An orphaned child whose own father I once cared for makes noise on the piano that makes my bones rattle. How is this going to end? Who is going to take care of me?*

And what do I do about the contents of the coat and hat that he has outgrown again? He is now a seventeen-year old young man and knows nothing about it or its contents. Just a schmatte, a rag to him. And when should he know? And how should I tell him?

Chapter 18
All Jazzed Up

Nikolai stood outside the shabby nightclub entrance, looking at a blank space above the door where the old sign had been. Below this was a fancy new replacement sign in blue and red and gold letters welcoming guests to the Cotton Club. He walked through the front door at 6 pm and steered around the tables and chairs toward the expansive bar. He asked the woman behind the bar if he could speak to the manager. She was a tall brunette. She had long curls that reached down her back and her sparkling silver headband pushed her hair off her face, revealing large brown eyes with long eyelashes. Nikolai could not take his eyes off her cleavage. She appeared scantily attired in a tight, white cotton blouse, half-sleeves, and around her neck was a gold chain with a single ruby red rhinestone that fell just to the right place. Nicolai noticed her bright red leather belt buckle, cinching her jet-black skirt. While Nikolai was eyeing the bottles of liquor lining the shelves behind the bar, he could not ignore her long legs as they disappeared beneath her abbreviated hem line. The woman leaned over the bar, brought her lit cigarette up to her crimson lips, inhaled a deep drag, and blew the smoke in Nikolai's eyes.

"Hey sonny, my eyes are up here," she cracked. "Now, what do you want?"

"My name is Nikolai Stein and I'm here to see the manager. I heard you need a piano player."

"Yeah, that's right. We do. So who are you?"

"I'm here to play the piano, ma'am." The woman scanned Nikolai from top to bottom; the soft dark curly hair, the deep blue eyes, the six-foot-one-inch frame, carrying a gentle quality that seemed to come through despite his street-boy clothing and self-effacing demeanor.

"I see," said the bartender. Silence. Nikolai stood there, not knowing what to say. The woman returned to setting up the bar, cigarette hanging from her lips, wiping down the counter as if the two had never spoken. Nikolai cleared his throat several times, hoping the woman would pay attention to him, or tell him what to do, or tell him where to go. As he waited in silence, a half-dozen young women, perhaps show girls, came out from the back somewhere or down the stairs and poured themselves a cup of coffee and lit their cigarettes at the far end of the bar before vanishing as quickly as they appeared. They barely gave Nikolai a glance. Finally, the brunette slowly walked over opposite Nikolai and said, "Well, if you're here to play, what are you waiting for?"

"Yeah, but don't you think I should talk to the manager?" asked Nikolai with a puzzled expression.

"Look, sonny. There's the boss, Charlie Solomon, and then there's me, Sophie. So, get over there and start playing."

"What do you want me to play?"

"Play me something nice and pretty, why don't you? We open the doors at 7:00."

With eyebrows raised, Nikolai turned on his heels and walked slowly over to the upright piano. After playing a number of scales, he noted that the piano was quite discordant, not nearly as in tune as Mr. Rosenberg's pianos. Soon, the soft and melodic tones of Bach's Goldberg variations carried throughout the room. Sophie stopped what she was doing behind the bar. She stared at the new piano man, took a deep breath, and said quietly, "That's the most beautiful thing I ever heard. You..."

Before she could finish her sentence, a young woman, maybe 19 or 20 came strutting out of the back room, wavy golden hair, soft hazel eyes, scantily clad in a green sequined flapper dress, smoking a Lucky Strike. She called out in a loud but sweet voice, two octaves above the music, "Hey Beethoven, why don't you jazz it up?"

Nikolai looked over his shoulder. He thought his heart stopped. He'd never seen anyone so beautiful. He stared at this loudmouth angel.

"Wow," Sophie yelled out. "Hey, Trixie, shut your trap and go back in your hole." Nikolai continued to stare. Trixie stood her ground at the end of the bar. Her lips starting to curl into a faint smile. Hands on her hips, she barked, "Well, what are you waiting for Mr. Piano Man?"

Nikolai slowly turned to the keyboard, loosened his shoulders, stretched his fingers, and played one of his favorites, "Drop Me Off in Harlem." The tune rolled off his fingertips as he played with his back to the beautiful Madonna who made the request. He felt like he was playing for the Queen. And when he finished with a flurry and turned around with his biggest smile, she was gone. Nikolai stared into space where the ghost had been.

He looked all around. Disappointed, he turned back to the piano and played until 6:55 pm. By this time Sophie had made herself up, had changed into a tight shiny teal flapper dress with a hem of silver beaded fringe. This was accessorized by a pearl choker and multiple silver bangles on each wrist. The ten or so other young waitresses/entertainers were finishing up their last cigarette or that final shot of whiskey before opening time. Nikolai stood from the piano bench, and walked over to the bar.

"Miss Sophie, before we start, can you tell me the hours and how much I'm getting paid?"

"Listen, Nick, you just start playing when the doors open up and keep playin' 'til they close. You get a five-minute break each hour. The boss will see you at the end of tonight and he'll let you know the score," closing her eyes, giving him a half curtsy, and turning her back to him.

***

As Nikolai was midway through his second set, the angelic blonde appeared from nowhere and stepped onto the platform near the piano. As the young woman gripped the stand-up microphone, she leaned over and said, "Hey, Mozart, do you know "All of Me"? Nikolai looked at her with his biggest smile and said, "Anything for you. And the name is Nick."

"OK, Nick. My name's really Miriam. They just call me Trixie here," she winked "Now hit it with a little zip."

Nikolai craned his neck so he could see her perform. Her voice was velvet. She finished her song to energetic applause. Before Nikolai could talk to her, she disappeared again into the back room. He played his heart out for a half-dozen singers until 2 am, exhausting his repertoire including everything from "Squeeze Me," "Ain't Misbehavin'," to "Black and Blue," "Turn on the Heat" and "Honeysuckle Rose." He got to play one more set with his Madonna, but received nothing but a thrown kiss at the end of her last song. The lights finally dimmed. The crowd and noise dissipated and Nikolai heard someone from the bar yell out, "OK, piano player. Night's over. The Boss wants to see you at the end of the bar and I wouldn't keep him waiting if you know what's good for you."

Nick rose from his seat and walked toward a tall, well-built gentleman at the far side of the bar, short dark hair, charcoal single-breasted suit, red club tie, white carnation in his lapel. He stubbed out his cigarette as his new player approached.

"Hey maestro, what's your name?

"Nicolai Stein."

"And who sent you over here?"

"Harold Shapiro."

"Where were you born, kid?

"Odessa."

"Is that so? Hmm. Listen up. You did good. Pay's 20 bucks a night. Be here Thursday, Friday, and Saturday nights. Seven o'clock 'till closing. One drink a night. Any more and you're out."

"OK, Mr. Solomon. Thank you. Mr. Solomon." King Solomon, with a smirk, half closed dark olive eyes, reached into his pocket and withdrew a wad of bills. He peeled a twenty-dollar bill off the top and shoved it at Nick who, wide eyed, grabbed the bill and shoved it in his pocket.

"Thank you, Mr. Solomon. Thank you very much."

"Now scram."

"Yes, sir."

As Nikolai turned and walked toward the exit, he heard a now recognizable voice shout, "And don't forget, boychik, the rest of the days you and Harry Shapiro will work together as a team. For me, and me only. I'll let you know how you can contribute."

But the young piano player was out the door, in the street, thinking only of his Aphrodite, his Bessie Smith, his Miriam.

Chapter 19
The King

Born in Russia in 1884, no one quite remembers much about Charles "King" Solomon's boyhood. His father, Joseph, settled the family in Salem, Massachusetts. It wasn't easy for Charlie and his brothers, growing up as immigrant Jewish boys in the seat of Puritan inquisition. Charlie was a loner, disliked by the guys, by the girls, by his elders, or anyone for that matter. He gravitated to the pool tables at his uncle's restaurant where he honed his skills. At fifteen, he took the train into Boston proper on the Eastern Railroad from Salem to East Boston where he hustled older guys in the city pool halls. He garnered a taste for fast money and fast women. As a teenager he experienced multiple arrests for illegal activities, including breaking and entering, gambling, narcotics dealing, and prostitution. By the next decade, however, he was on his way to controlling prostitution, gambling, and narcotics not only in Boston but in all of New England. He acquired theaters, nightclubs, restaurants, and hotels in Boston, New York, and Montreal for his racketeering empire. He commanded liquor distribution in a large swath of the northeastern corner of the country. As Prohibition washed over the nation in 1920, the Al Capone of Boston was poised to control his rackets kingdom with no serious threats. His powerful jaws opened wide, swallowed, and spit out those immigrants desperate for a piece of the action, yearning to join the club with money in their pocket, hoping to be somebody in the new world, no matter the risk.

***

"You playing tonight?" asked Harold Shapiro, as he drove Nikolai in his used Ford Model T toward the South Boston waterfront.

"Yeah. Pay's good and I get to do the thing I like to do the best," said Nikolai, shifting in the seat wearing his pleated grey flannels and shined wingtips.

"Like watching that Miriam of yours, you mean?"

"That too," said Nikolai, head remaining perfectly still, eyes shifting to the left toward the driver.

"You and her are getting along pretty good, I hear." Howard shifted his eyes toward his partner in crime, a smirk on his face.

"Hey, look here Harold. I asked you to keep your mouth shut about that. I've thanked you plenty for lending me your car. Got you that showgirl too. Nobody's to know right now. We've got plans, Miriam and me. We gotta wait. That's all. In fact, you oughta try it yourself, instead of hanging out with those *kurveh* at Charlie's cathouses."

"OK. OK. To each his own. All's I'm saying is Mr. Solomon don't like people having plans, if you know what I mean."

"For now, I'll settle for walking her home and being with her every show night. She's got a place with three other girls at the club." Harold cleared his throat and adjusted himself in the driver's seat.

"So how's Sophie? And how's Mr. Solomon treating you?"

"They let me be, most of the time. But hey, the dough that flows through that place and all his joints is incredible."

"Yeah? How much ya' figure?"

"I don't know, maybe 10,000 bucks a night. Maybe more."

Harold drove them down to the docks, home of the fish markets, the seafood restaurants, the wharf where the boats came in, the trucks that picked up and distributed the catch for the day—cod, haddock, redfish, flounder, pogy and other groundfish--throughout New England and New York. The South Boston waterfront was one of many stops that Solomon's two bagmen made together, collecting a protection tax, day in and day out. Nikolai was starting to get the hang of the trade.

Over the last six months, Nikolai got to know the shopkeepers, the truck drivers, and especially the boatmen. Fish did not seem to be the only product delivered by sea, particularly at night. Occasionally, the bosses ordered Nikolai and Harold to supervise the unloading of the cases of rum from Canada, the Bahamas and the Caribbean. One night when the two were on their way home from organizing the liquor drop-offs, Harold shoved a paper bag across the front seat into Nikolai's ribs.

"Hey. What the fuck is this?"

"I think you'll be needing this. It's getting dangerous out there." Nikolai pulled out a handgun. Heavier than expected. He sat frozen in the passenger seat.

"It's a snub nose 38."

He was almost 18, and he'd only laid eyes on a gun twice in his life. He had forgotten those moments. Blocked them out. Once, when as a boy in the old country, he found the Remington Colt 1890 Revolver under his father's pillow. Wide-eyed and afraid, he had heard by then whispers and innuendoes of the activities of his father, The Fox, and his friends. The second time was when his Uncle Sasha came running into the house, rifle in hand, bending to hug him, telling him someone shot his father.

"They call it a bulldog. A little tough to shoot but easy to carry and conceal."

"Holy shit, Harold. What the hell is this for?

"Look, up 'til now, most of our visits have been pretty smooth. Not much trouble. You know I still make the rounds on days that you're playin'. But you are older, and bigger, and stronger now, and you should know that things get rough once in a while."

"Yeah, I know," said Nikolai. "A couple of shoves here and there. A few unfortunate words. But a gun?"

"Look, Charlie Solomon insists. Some of those Gustin Irish assholes have been sniffin' around. Believe me, it's better to send a bullet than to receive a bullet." The Gustin Gang was the Irish outfit from South Boston, run by Frank Wallace. The competition between Solomon and Wallace in the early decades of the twentieth century in Boston was fierce and deadly, particularly over liquor and narcotics.

A gun. The next step. Consciously or unconsciously, Nikolai felt his life making a deadly and serious turn. A notch up. He was making more money than he had before, enough so he could afford more food and clothes and a better home for Natalya. But… "And you better not let your grandmother see that thing. How is she anyway? I saw her at the market a few weeks ago. She's getting really old, Nikolai."

***

"Who's complaining, my Nikolai? Who am I to ask where or how we can afford these chickens, the corned beef, the breads…pastries no less? I'm glad to cook for you, but does this noise you make on the piano pay you so well that you can afford all this?"

"Don't worry, Grandma. I'm making good money now."

"Well, maybe with your two jobs, playing piano for that nice Mr. Rosenberg and that hoodlum Mr. Solomon. I hope you know what you're doing. I worry constantly. And don't think I don't know about that Miriam girl. Miriam Lewinski. I know Mrs. Shultz from the synagogue. And she's friends with Mrs. Cokin. Mrs. Cokin's brother-in-law Saul Shalowitz has a sister Rebecca Lewinski married to Sam Lewinski. Their daughter ran away to become a showgirl, you know, singer and a dancer. *Shana punum* people say."

"She's a nice girl, Grandma."

"Oy, Nikolai, I'm getting too old for this. How long am I going to be around? What happens if someone breaks your fingers? You can't play that devil's music anymore. Ever think of that? Then what are we going to do? Believe me, God, I worry about you. Never mind, I worry about me!"

"No one's going to break my fingers, Grandma."

"Oh, no. You, hanging around that Harold Shapiro, once the savior of the New World, now a hoodlum working for hoodlums, and you…we might as well go back to Preobrajenska street. One step forward, two steps back. Your father, God rest his soul."

"Grandma, haven't I gotten us a better flat…two bedrooms, second floor, our own bathroom and kitchen? Yeah, it's small but we have heat and hot water."

"Yes. It's better. And I love you for this. But I want better for you. I hear you've gotten pretty fond of that singing nightingale of yours. How are you going to support her… and me?"

Nikolai no longer worked for Mr. Rosenberg. Working for Charles Solomon took up all his time, between piano playing, shaking down businesses and shop owners, and spending as much time as he could with Miriam. He had no time. *Wait. Natalya didn't know. Did she?*

"And now that we have a little extra food, wouldn't you know, you don't eat. You're too skinny."

She was right. He hadn't been eating well. He felt anxious, pressured, apprehensive about the new life he was living. Of course, he would not trade it for the world…playing three shifts a week for Miriam, his infatuation turning to true love for this creature. These last few months, the plans they made, dreams they had, player and singer. But he needed time. He needed some luck. But most of all, he needed money.

Chapter 20
Elope

"Come on. Get in," said Nick in the dark of night, a warm summer breeze blowing in from the west. Nick opened the passenger door to the black Ford Model T. Light blue valise in hand, Miriam squealed, "Oh, thank you sir." She kissed Nick wetly on the lips, stepped up on the running board, and into the machine. Bucking and sputtering, the automobile moved slowly down the street, toward Route 20, and out of town.

"Hey Nicky, sure was nice of Harold to lend you his car," said Miriam nervously.

"Yeah. And he gave me a lesson or two on how to drive it. I bought six cans of gas to get us to Worcester and back."

"And you're sure this rabbi of yours in Worcester can marry us?"

"Don't worry. It's all set. By this time tomorrow, you'll be Mrs. Nikolai Stein," said Nick proudly, big smile on his sweaty face but jitters in his chest.

"Yeah, and that Dottie Diamond will be sorry. I'm so mad at her. Can you imagine? Her and Sam Medoff were supposed to elope with us, but half way down the ladder from her bedroom, she calls it off and tells Sam she's not doing it. Huh!"

"Yeah, well that's their tough luck. 'Specially when they hear we're moving to New York."

"Nicky, tell me again about how we're going to move to New York and get jobs as a team…you playing the ivories and me singing and dancing."

"I told you. I've been listening to Fats Waller, Art Tatum, and Lil Hardin Armstrong on my Victrola. I get to hear Bessie Smith and Ma Rainey once in a while on one of those radios that Mr. Solomon has."

"And what about the nightclubs, Nicky?"

"Are you kidding? We're going to play in clubs like the 43 in Soho, the Stork Club and the Club Intime. Maybe we can even join one of those bands that come through here like Duke Ellington, Louie Armstrong, or

Paul Whiteman's Band. They pay big. Five times as much as Charlie does." They drove steadily westward on the long dark road.

"Gee, Nick, I'm so excited but scared at the same time."

"Yeah, me too. But what do we gotta be scared about?

"I don't know but my heart's beatin' a mile a minute."

"Listen. We got nothin' to be scared of. I love you. You love me. What else is there?"

"You're right. Hey Nicky, are we really going to stay in a hotel?"

"Oh, yeah. I told you. We're staying at a famous joint owned by our own Boston Charlie. Fancy. We'll stay all night 'til it's time to come home tomorrow. Harold wants his car back tomorrow night. You know. Business the next morning."

"And how do you know this rabbi again?"

"He's a friend of the family in the old country. He married my parents in Odessa where I was born. I think my parents even had him do my bris."

"Now that's a close family friend if I ever heard of one," said Miriam. She looked over at her man, who was desperately trying to keep the Model-T steady.

"You know I love you, Nikolai Stein." She grabbed his thigh.

"I love you more, babe," said Nick.

He thought about his father, The Fox. He would not relate many of the stories he'd heard about his father, Uncle Mikhail, and their cronies to his new bride. Nicky took his hand off of the steering wheel for a moment and felt nervously for the ring in his pocket. He wished he could afford a bigger ring. But he couldn't. And what about kids? He couldn't think about that now. He needed more money. A lot more. He'd speak to Charlie Solomon, again.

Chapter 21
Protection Taxes

"We have a few stops in East Boston today," said Harold as he drove the car from Bremen Street and crossed over to Bennington Street. Nikolai jumped out to collect from Irving's Bakery. No problem. They stopped at Arnold's, the scrap dealer, always a worry given the two German Shepherd attack dogs protecting the entrance. Harold jumped out, tossing a sausage at each canine. Made the job easier. He was never worried much about collecting on the East Boston waterfront. A few years back a massive fire gutted this neighborhood. It was so destructive that many of the Easties relocated to Dorchester and Roxbury. No one knew what or who started the fire. Harold knew. Rumors flew. No one was charged but Solomon's gang did nothing to quell the gossip. After that, every shop owner in East Boston paid his monthly dues.

Still, no self-respecting businessman was happy about these monthly shakedowns either. No one thought it was OK. Their fathers before them had enough of this bullshit back in the old country. This was America. Work hard. Build your own future with nobody on your back--or hand in your pocket.

Harold climbed back in the car, clanked it in gear, and drove slowly down Bennington Street until they arrived about a block from Prescott Street. He stopped, put on the brake, and kept the car idling. Like the keys of his piano, Nikolai was very familiar with Bennington Street. He knew every store, every alley, every shop owner, every intersecting street. Without looking out his passenger window, he knew Harold had stopped in front of Mr. Rosenberg's Music Store.

"Hey, asshole," said Nikolai, feeling the hot flush rising from his tailbone to the roots of his hair. "What are you stopping here for?"

"So you can get out and collect from your old friend."

"I'm not collecting a damn thing from Mr. Rosenberg and neither are you."

"Well, somebody's got to do it. King Solomon don't like people who don't ante up. And when Mr. Solomon don't like something, it ain't good for us."

"I don't give a shit what Solomon likes or doesn't like. Now move this junk heap."

Harold stared at Nikolai momentarily, opened his door leaving it ajar, eased out of his seat, ambled toward the music store, and walked through the door. Nikolai sat there for a minute, face flushed, fists in a ball. Thoughts careened through his head like a hummingbird trapped in a cage. He couldn't see anyone through the showroom window. Just his grands and his baby grands, his classic and barrel organs. Not *his*, but temporarily gifted to him once, by a kind and generous music man...a man who had given him a shot, who had offered him a place in the New World.

Nikolai forced the car door open and stepped out. Stomach tight, thoughts on fire, he hustled toward the piano shop, through the door, and beelined through the showroom. Just then, Nikolai saw the shadow of a slight figure, now shuffling backward, being forced from the back room out into the rear of the main gallery. Nick stopped short. Harold emerged, shoving the store owner again, well past the threshold between the dark back office into the bright open expanse of the showroom.

The bagman raised his fist in the air and threatened Mr. Rosenberg.

"Listen, old man. Pay up or I'll shut you up. I'm not going to ask you again. Just give me my usual envelope and I'll be on my way."

"Tell you what," said Hyman Rosenberg, standing five feet away in his three-piece suit, beads of sweat forming on his brow, a trickle of blood from his right nostril.

"I'm going to give you *bubkis,* nothing. So what are you going to do, hit me again?"

"Harold, leave him alone. Let's go. Now, you asshole," yelled Nikolai, facing the back of Harold. "And I mean it. Turn around and walk away. Or I'm telling you, you're gonna be sorry."

"Oh yeah. Who says?" grunted Harold, stepping menacingly toward the old man.

"I say," blurted Rosenberg through his clenched teeth. He stood facing Harold, hands shaking as he pointed a gun in front of him that he pulled from his suit coat.

It all happened so fast. The sequence wasn't clear. Out of the corner of his eye, Nikolai saw Harold sneak a gun from his right coat pocket. A voice. No, a scream. From outside his body. "No…oooo." An explosion. His ears rang. Nikolai pulled the gun from his waistband. At that exact moment, Nikolai extended his right arm in front of him. The gun jerked backward, smoking. Harold staggered, and as he turned around, Nikolai scanned his pale, bewildered expression just before another blast rang out. A wild shot from who knew where? And then a third shot. Harold crumpled to the ground. Nikolai raised his eyes toward Hyman Rosenberg, feeling faint, heart hammering, comprehending the chaotic scene. The old man grimaced, groaned, placed his hand to his bleeding chest and slumped over, landing face first upon the keyboard of a mahogany Bosendorfer Concert Grand 290 Imperial.

Chapter 22
The Aftermath

Nikolai froze in place. He felt like the wind got knocked out of him. A gnawing in the pit of his stomach. A sudden chill. Just for a moment. No thought. No plan. He robotically turned around and ran out of the store, jumped into the driver's seat, slammed the door, and drove off. *Where to? Which way?*

He drove to nowhere, until he found the car driving toward Miriam's place, several blocks from the club. He parked the car on the street, hustled out, and ran up three flights to Miriam's flat.

"Miriam, Miriam," Nick yelled, knock, knock, knocking on the door. "Let me in," again knocking harder on the door. The door opened a crack and Miriam stuck her head through the opening that the chain allowed. Flinching back, she could see her husband drenched with sweat, pale as a snowshoe hare, actually trembling as he said, "Miriam, Miriam. Thank God you're here."

She opened the door wider. Nick padded in, pacing back and forth. She'd never seen him like this.

"Nicky, what's the matter? You look like you've just seen Jack the Ripper."

"Miriam, look, are any of the other girls home?"

"No, they're working. But Lisa will be home soon. What's happening? Why do you look so scared? And… Jesus, is that a gun?" she said, looking at the waistband of his trousers. Still panting, Nick told Miriam what happened.

"Oy yoy yoy, Nicky. What are we going to do?"

"For now, we are going to go to work as usual." He looked at his beautiful wife, a little fuller than just a week ago. "As it is, you may not be able to work for much longer."

"Listen, Nicky, a couple of girdles can take a girl pretty far. But you're right…a couple of months…maybe?"

"Listen, I'm going to stash the car behind your building for now. I'm going to play at the club as usual tonight."

Nick attacked those black and white keys as best he could that night. What to do with the car? The gun? How was Miriam going to cope? What would Mr. Solomon say?

He was worried for his life…Miriam's life…their baby's life. He couldn't clear his head. The more he tried to review his situation, the harder he pounded on the piano. At one point, Sophie the bartender yelled over, "Hey, Mozart, try not to crack the white keys. You can't just play the black ones, y'know."

Nick couldn't wait to leave. He played his last set, downed two fingers of bourbon neat, and rushed for the door.

"Hey, wait a damn minute. Where the hell do you think you're going?" shouted Sophie.

"Charlie wants to see you…in the back…now."

***

Nick stood in front of the King…dark brown double-breasted suit, red and yellow club tie, yellow pocket square, extinguishing his cigarette as he began. The two stood facing each other in the tiny smoke-filled back room. Charlie's face was stern. Ricky Darman, his body guard, stood in the corner beside the floor lamp.

"So, Nick, I heard you've gotten yourself a new car. Mazel Tov."

"Yes, sir. I've been meaning to talk to you," said Nick.

"Let's not beat around the bush, alright son."

"Mr. Solomon?"

"Listen, I catch wind of everything. So, don't bullshit me. What happened in East Boston?" Nick told his story to the boss.

"So, I heard two shots. I ran in and it looked like the old man pulled a gun on Harold. They shot and killed each other. They were both not movin'. I ran out of there. Harold left his machine idling. I drove out of there in a flash."

Solomon lit up another Lucky Strike and took a long drag. He exhaled the smoke in Nick's face, looking him over, up and down.

"Did anybody see you?"

"I don't know. I don't think so."

"Listen, you still got your gun?" Without waiting for a response, he said, "Get rid of it. Throw it into the Charles. You park the car behind my place, the Essex Hotel." Pause.

"You played good tonight. The clientele like you. So do the girls. Now scram. And watch your ass."

"Yes, Mr. Solomon," but as Nick turned to leave, he turned back to the King and said, "Look, boss. I gotta make more money. I take care of my grandmother. My girl and me…well we're getting on. I got a car now. You know I'm reliable. How 'bout more…uh, more responsibility? And maybe I should keep the gun…or a different gun. I'll still play for you if that's what you want?"

Solomon looked straight into Nick's eyes. He then looked across the room at Nooky Abrams, his second in command, leaning in the far corner. He stepped out of the shadows. Nickolai gripped tightly to the top of the chair in front of him to keep from trembling.

"More money means more risk, kid. Are you sure you're up to it?"

"Definitely."

"Nooky, talk to this boychik on Monday about the rum runs. Let's see what he can do. If he does his job at the wharves like he plays those keys, maybe he'll even work out. Now, get out of here, kid. Don't worry about your friend Harold. Nooky will get you a new gun. And take good care of that Miriam of yours."

Chapter 23
A Full Plate

Nikolai's horizons were expanding. He was still playing at the Cotton Club but the King had him playing at The Nuttings-on-the-Charles in Waltham as well. His notoriety on the piano was expanding and his exposure to visiting bands like Duke Ellington, Louis Armstrong, and Paul Whiteman thrilled and motivated him. Surprise accompaniments by the likes of Johnny Hodges and Harry Carney, born and raised in Cambridge and Boston, riveted him every time.

Miriam was starting to show. Two bodices were no longer up to the challenge.

"Y'know, Sophie says I'm going to have to stop singing and dancing sooner or later," she said to Natalya. "Maybe sooner." Miriam had moved in with Nick and Natalya. A tight squeeze again.

"So what? Don't worry yourself," said Natalya. "A beautiful girl like you will find work somewhere else. Pregnant or not, who wouldn't want a nice girl like you working for them? Who wants to work for that *ganef* [thief] Solomon anyway?"

"Well, maybe you're right. But I will need a job where I can also be there for you when you need me, Natalya," said Miriam.

"Don't worry. Grandma's a tough bird," grinned Nikolai.

"My Nikolai, even a tough fowl molts at some point. I'm old and have already seen too much. I'm mostly worried about you two now. And God knows what happened to old Green Eyes, our Harold. I hear things, you know."

"Well, luckily Mr. Solomon has doubled my salary. We'll all be OK for now. Speaking of work, I'm going out and I'll be back late. Don't wait up. I love you both," as he slammed the door behind him.

Never mind three. There soon would be four in the small flat. While he was excited for the new baby, he was feeling the pressure. Another mouth to feed. A child to clothe and care for. And physically, did he have some form of Couvade syndrome, or were his symptoms of nausea, weight gain, and sleeplessness a function of his new lifestyle? Natalya, who raised him, brought him to this country, supported him unconditionally, never interrogated him, was getting old and requiring more help. Thank goodness for Miriam's kindness toward her.

***

For the last six months, when he wasn't banging on the ivories at the clubs, Nick spent the other nights of the week at the beaches, at the docks, at any port convenient for King Solomon's liquor and drug-laden boats to smuggle in and run.

"Well, I guess that's all for tonight, Al. The trucks are all loaded and ready to go," said Nick. He stood relived on Winthrop Beach Road, flashlight in hand, watching the moon peek just over the sand dunes on the coast of southern Massachusetts. The sea breeze was still chilly and the gulls were quiet in the salty ocean night air.

"Yeah, those trucks will be going all over New England to make their deliveries before Easter," sighed Al, Nickolai's partner.

"Starting to warm up a bit, thank God. And thank God the cops have been layin' off us this winter. Haven't given us much trouble lately," said Nick.

"We had an incident at Orient Heights Beach a month ago, but Eddy paid the cops a hunk of change so they'd look the other way. Some of that Chinese comin' in with the booze. China to England then over to here."

"Wow, close call. Lots going on now, that's for sure. All over. That freakin' war in France is still ragin'. Three and a half years now. Who knows when that will end?

Yeah, and how 'bout those assholes in Congress closin' in on that fuckin' national Prohibition Act or some shit. People are twitchy."

"On top of all that, those Russian bastards are now starting some sort of revolution over there. The Boss ain't really worried. Fact is, he says it's going to be better for us if they approve that Prohibition shit. Word is that King Solomon has fleets of boats pickin' up the stuff from Europe, Canada, and the Caribbean and bringing it in at thirty different spots on the coasts of New Jersey, Long Island, and New England."

"Yeah, and better not let Charlie find out you touched one bottle, one box, or one bag of nothin."

"That's for sure."

"Yeah, well tomorrow night then, Al?"

"Revere Beach, right? Midnight?"

"Course there's more than liquor in that shipment. Some of that Chinese heroin shit."

"Yeah, I heard. Come on, jump in, I'll give you a lift home."

They drove home hoping that the entire order got delivered. They couldn't afford any screw-ups. One mistake and maybe you wouldn't be around anymore. Nooky had eyes in the back of his head and everywhere else. Who knew where the retribution would come from—the boss, the local police, the government, their competitors?

Nick thought about what Al said about the Prohibition thing. As the war in Europe ground on, the rise in anti-German sentiment was all over the streets, the papers, the workplace, and anywhere that people drank. Many of the breweries had German names. Colonists had been drinking since they set foot in the New World. Yet the temperance movement took hold in the latter part of the nineteenth century and Wayne Wheeler's Anti-Saloon League held on like a proverbial bulldog. Not that an anti-alcohol law would be bad for business. In fact, with the network he had set up, Charles Solomon couldn't wait for the government to bring it on. Nick's job would grow riskier. More complicated. The heat would come down harder on the guys meeting the boats, organizing the truck loadings, and deliveries. And the drivers themselves, always wondering if the next curve was hiding a state police roadblock.

Word was that King Solomon was tight with the Bronfmans in Canada...Montreal, Quebec. The Solomon and Bronfman families had escaped from the anti-Semitic pogroms in the Russian Empire, the latter from Moldova. This old country connection would benefit the Boss of Boston for decades.

***

Natalya sat at the small wooden table in the kitchen, drinking her coffee, nibbling on a sugar cube. As Nikolai entered from the bedroom she said, "I didn't hear you come home last night. Or this morning, I should say."

"Yeah, the Boss has me runnin' all over the place."

The pale old woman sat hunched over, wrapped in her black shawl, her white hair dipping into her steaming cup.

"And shooting all over the place?"

"What? No. No shooting, Grandma."

"That's not what I hear."

"Pays the bills, at least."

"Not all of them, I'm afraid," said Natalya. "Yes, it's getting warmer as spring comes, but we're behind on the coal payments. But never mind me. I feel like I'm back in Odessa when Anatoly and I first took your father in on that awful day. That was then and this is now. But this is no way for your wife to live. And the baby's coming soon."

"I'll soon make more money. We'll move to a better place. The Boss says he has big plans for me."

"Boss, schmoss. Mr. Big Bully. And suppose his plans make it so you don't come home one night. Something happens to you. What's going to happen to your wife, your child…to me, Mr. Big Shot?"

"Nothin's going to happen to me, Grandma."

Natalya used the table to push herself up, groaning, knees cracking, and walked over to the singular dresser. From the bottom drawer she withdrew a child's jacket, dark tan suede, lamb's wool interior, abalone buttons, and a child's cap to match. She shuffled back to the table, plunked down on the wooden chair, and motioned Nikolai to come closer.

"Please sit, my Nikolai, my grown man. You remember this coat that you wore as a boy?…A sad boy in Odessa, a bewildered boy crossing Asia, a growing boy in America, a parentless boy in a new world?"

"Sure, I remember that old thing. I hated wearing the hat."

"Your true grandmother, Maria Galina Schteinkov, sewed these for your father, for you, for your son, and for his son."

"She actually thought these schmatas would last for generations?"

"My Nikolai, how do you think your Uncle Mikhail arranged for our escape? Our journey from Odessa, to Moldova, to Hamburg, to America…a life in Boston? So many people had to be bribed…wagon drivers, truck drivers, riverboat men, innkeepers, sea captains. They risked their lives to help Jews." She looked up inquisitively at her boychik, now a man, with a lilt to her head and eyebrows stretched to the ceiling.

"Here, feel this," she said, taking his hand and forcing it gently around something hard and round in the bottom coat lining.

"Uh-huh. And here," she said guiding his fingers over the other two large bumps in the band of the old hat.

"*Vas ist das*? What is this?" he asked. She couldn't remember when he last spoke Yiddish. His ears pulled slightly back as Natalya pulled a thread near one of the lumps. Onto the table tumbled a sparkling diamond as big as a walnut. The gem rolled and stopped right in front of Nikolai. Wide eyed. Mouth ajar. Speechless. Natalya sat with the coat and hat in her lap. She too stared at the faceted rock.

"How do you think I afforded my beautiful house that you'd come to visit as a boy--white picket fence, chickens in the yard, forest in the back?" whispered Natalya.

"You'd make those round cookies," Nikolai said softly. "The dough of flour and water and butter and sugar, and you'd have me push my thumb into the middle… like this, Grandma… and you'd fill them with my favorite jam…thumb cookies we'd call them."

"Your father, at just about your age, eighteen I'd say, gave me and Anatoly a diamond like this one, from this very coat. We had nothing…dirt floors, rats…"

"And you have saved these here, in that drawer, this whole time?" Nikolai stared at Natalya. His eyelids were nearly closed, at first a blush of confusion, disorientation, perhaps anger that quickly melted into gratitude, and even reverence for this old soul who had kept things afloat for all these years. Hesitantly, Nikolai muttered, "So what are we going to do? What should we do? We've had them all this time?"

"The diamonds are yours to do what you want to do with them. You will know."

"But why now? Why haven't you told me of this before? I am about to have a child of my own. Three generations."

"I thought there would be a time to tell you and a time that would be not so good. Your Grandmother Schteinkov knew that there would be times that you would need these gifts."

"Does Miriam know?"

"The hat and coat will be in that drawer as they have been. I'm sure you'll know what to do and what to say and to whom to say it," she said with tears in her eyes. Natalya kissed her Nikolai on the forehead, the son of The Fox, of Moyshe-Yakov Schteinkov, of the bereaved boy who she took in and raised so many years ago. She folded the pair, stood up with a wince and a groan, and placed the garments back in the left-hand corner of the old bureau.

Chapter 24
No Choice

When Nicky showed her the contents of the jacket and the hat, her eyes bulged like Barney Google. Miriam Lewinski Stein had only seen a diamond in a jewelry store case. Just looking. Except for Betty Jaransky's at the club when she got engaged to Roger. A tiny one. She could hardly see it, but she told Betty it was beautiful, anyway. Of course, Nicky bought her an engagement ring, a small round ruby with a pearl on each side. *That's all we can afford, after all.*

She was eight months pregnant. In a nice way, her boss Sophie basically told Miriam that she "kinda didn't want her hanging around the club at this point."

"Come back later," she said. "Good luck with the baby," she said.

The flat was cramped already. It was cold. It was too hard to keep clean. And the constant screaming of the Morrises…all five of them. Maybe. Just maybe. Why couldn't they use one of those big diamonds to move to the suburbs? Why wait for a rainy day? The baby will need fresh air. And maybe (his? her?) own baby's room? And Natalya? Maybe a yard to sit in the sun? Maybe a little garden?

Miriam would have to talk to Nicky when he got home tonight. Or maybe tomorrow morning.

***

He worked from Rockport to Plymouth. Maybe Nick had bitten off more than he could chew. While Nick handled the imports primarily, Charles Solomon Inc. was heavily involved in gambling, prostitution, bail bonding, nightclubs, and of course liquor and narcotics distribution. Nick felt OK about working with the rum runners…the pickups, the deliveries, the payoffs, and the bribes. He was always glad when the shipment was pure liquor, like tonight, at Orient Heights. Things usually went smoother that way… no angst, nerves weren't as frayed. He'd meet Al and the others there at midnight.

It was the heroin that made him uncomfortable. He was going to have to talk with the Boss

***

The Irish Boston cops could rationalize the bribes they took to look the other way when it came to offshore liquor deliveries. But for some reason the dope coming in through their port of Boston went right up their collective ass. It offended them somehow. Or maybe it offended their mothers? Who knew? Sometimes, somehow, the local police knew when one of Charlie's shipments was tainted with the white powder. "I know what you mean, Mr. Wallace," said the sergeant with the Irish brogue. "My men appreciate your information and your generosity."

Frank Wallace and his enforcer brother Steve (an ex-Olympic boxer) were Southies (South Boston) who represented stiff competition. They'd been hijacking beer shipments for years…shipments that belonged to Solomon and his Jews, and now to Joe Lombardi and Phil Buccola and "them I-talians" who were moving in big time.

"We don't like that shit comin' into this country any more than you do. We worry about the kids, our families, our own kind," grumbled Sergeant O'Connell.

"Yeah, you've got my word on this one. The Jew Man's taking a big shipment at Revere Beach," said Wallace. "Tomorrow night. You think I want Chinese shit comin' through Boston? I appreciate you understanding, Sarge."

"And we appreciate you and your brother's donations to the precinct and to St. Michael's," said the sergeant.

"No problem. We take care of our own kind. You can bet on that," said the leader of the Gustin Gang, the earliest Irish American gang in Boston before and during Prohibition.

***

"Who the hell said it was getting warmer with Spring around the corner? It's colder than Siberia out here. At least we have the full moon," said Al. Nick arrived with his collar up against the cold wind, hands in his pockets. He was aggravated. He had to walk way the hell down the beach road. All the guys had parked closer. Their trucks blocked the road down to the jetty. He had to park his car behind some gigantic boulders left over from the construction of the quay when Revere Beach was designed as the first public beach in the country. He always preferred to pull his car up to the front of the action so he could direct the shipments, pay the men, and organize the product.

The guys saw the blinking lights offshore–three quick flashes–the sign that the boats were coming ashore to deliver their payload.

"Could do without this howling wind. Let's go, boys. Load 'em up," yelled Al. For the next two hours, the ten men hauled the heavy oak crates of liquor weighing maybe 40 pounds and the more plentiful lighter cases of pure heroin packed in bulk. The strong wind blowing in from the Atlantic did not help the loading job. If not for that 30-knot wind blowing sand off the dunes, the men might have heard engines idling in the distance, some dogs whimpering. Or seen a headlight or two being extinguished. Perhaps the silhouette of a paddy wagon.

"Easy peasy, Nick. All the guys know their drop-off points," said Al as Nick paid the drivers. They climbed into their trucks, a few engines started when …all hell broke loose. Sirens blaring, headlights blazing, whistles blowing, crowds of policemen yelling, charging. No way out. One-way beach road.

"Holy shit!"

"What the fuck!"

"Motherfucker!"

Confused men ran in all directions. Some down the road. Some onto the beach. A few jumped into the waves. The cops ran, billy clubs in one hand, pistols in the other. Shots echoed on both sides. The Solomon boys ran in the dark, along the crescent of the beach toward the Pier Dancing Pavilion, chased by the hounds of Boston's Finest. There was nowhere to hide in the moonlight. Their fate was incontrovertible.

Nick ran the opposite way. Against the chaotic flow. He moved stealthily toward the only vehicle parked at the far end of the road, in back of the huge rocks. *Behind enemy lines*, thought Nick. From boulder to boulder, in the shadows, from the pavilion to the beach shack, he heard the haunting distant gunshots, the dogs barking, both captors and captives screaming. He reached his car, started the engine, and without headlights slowly drove back down the beach lane toward the main road. The wind had picked up and swayed his Model-T from side to side. *Need to get away. Need to get away.* Nothing else mattered. No other thoughts.

He drove west. And drove and drove. Out of Boston, past Sommerville, Waltham, Cambridge, Framingham. No stopping. As fast as he dared. The winds died down. His gas gauge showed near empty. Nick drove until he reached his destination at the end of Main Street in Worcester at 4 in the morning.

***

Nikolai awoke in a strange bed, in a strange house. Still fully dressed, he climbed out of bed, walked out of the unfamiliar bedroom into a great room dominated by a long, weathered oak table surrounded by eight wooden chairs. At the head of the table was a mug of steaming coffee. Alongside the mug were a white piece of paper, a pen, and an accompanying stamped envelope. The Rabbi stood looking out the window on the right side of the front door. His back was to Nikolai. It was raining.

"Uh hmm," the Rabbi cleared his throat, standing in his black robe, still facing the window.

"Rabbi," said Nikolai. "Thank you for letting me stay the night."

"Of course," said the cleric. "Have your coffee. How's your wife?"

Nikolai grabbed the coffee mug, took a loud sip, and walked over to his host.

"Rabbi, my wife is fine. She's eight months pregnant. What are you looking at so intently?"

"There, across the street. They're calling you." Nikolai, a confused look on his face, now stood side by side with the rabbi who married him and Miriam.

"What do you mean? Who's calling me?" Nikolai feared the law had already caught up with him.

"Mr. James Montgomery Flagg and his creation, Uncle Sam."

Nikolai followed his gaze across the street where a man-sized sidewalk poster stood framed in red. The picture was of an old white-haired man, white goatee, dressed in a blue overcoat, white rumpled button-down shirt, red bow tie, featuring piercing, menacing eyes. The poster figure had a grey top hat with a blue band studded with white stars, as he pointed outward at any passerby with his long bony finger. The beseeching sign read:

"I WANT YOU FOR US ARMY"

Just behind the poster stood the Army Recruiting Office.

"No choice," said the Rabbi, still facing forward.

"Rabbi, are you suggesting that I enlist in the army?"

"No choice. You mumbled quite a bit to me before you fell asleep last night. No choice."

"But I have work, my wife, my Grandmother Natalya, a baby due any week now."

"No choice, son. They'll find you here. There are no secrets. I'll talk to our people in Boston about Miriam and Natalya. I will see to your car until you get back, God willing. And your gun," glancing at Nikolai for the first time. Silence.

"But Rabbi, I can't just join the army. They'll ship me overseas. I'm trying to make a life for myself."

"Why don't you sit down at the table and write the letter to your wife?"

"Letter? What letter? asked Nikolai.

"The letter saying you have no choice. You'll know what to write. And time is wasting the longer we *kibbitz*."

Nikolai stared at the Rabbi. He then stared across Main Street. His chest tightened as if bound by hawser rope. His fingers turned cold. He thought about his predicament. His brow furrowed until it hurt. His head throbbed. Nikolai turned from the window and planted himself at the table. He slowly picked up the pen, looked off into nowhere, and wrote.

PART III

Chapter 25
Overseas

The first letter stunned her. A nightmare. She'd been dreading the worst. Frightened. Expecting him to walk through the door at any moment. Lots of crying. Baby kicking. No Nicky. Terrifying.

Dearest Miriam,
I think I played one note too many this time. We had a disastrous night at Revere Beach last night. You might read about it in the paper. While I was lucky to get away, the law is after me, and my choices are slim to none. I will not be returning home soon, but I will write and let you know how I am. I have joined the US Army. No choice. I will come back to you. I promise. You will have Natalya to take care of you during the birth of our beautiful child, as she cared for me and my father before that.
Take my Grandmother Schteinkov's hat and coat and use them to buy you and the baby and Natalya a nice home in Newton, or Waltham, or Brookline. Rabbi Lipschitz, who married us, will help you get settled in whatever town you decide to live. He'll know the rabbi wherever you move to, I'm sure..
I love you with all my heart and hope to be back in your arms before you know it.
Love,
Nicky
April 15, 1918.

Dearest Miriam,
We'll be shipping out for Best, France, tomorrow. I'll write when I get to Gai Paris. Kisses to you and to Moses (Moishie) Yakov Stein.
Love,
Nicky

June 15, 1918

Miriam sat in the living room of their new home in Newton, breast feeding the new little man in her life. She could hear Natalya humming to herself while she sat in the new glass-enclosed sunroom.

***

Dearest Miriam,

Two weeks ago, we disembarked in Best, France. We first traveled by train to Paris. Of course, we did not receive the momentous reception that General John J. Pershing and his A.E.F. did when they arrived on July 4, 1917, heralded as saviors, a symbol of deliverance from a war with no end. The French are fatigued by four years of war. The thing is that while in the US people are playing the piano, drinking booze, and out at nightclubs, the French are holding on for dear life, saving and scraping, and losing loved ones and their homes. Now that my birthright Russia has sought an armistice with our enemy, it has allowed the Germans to transfer nearly fifty divisions to the Western Front.

Within a day of arriving in Paris, we were sent four hours by train close to Neufchateau. They ordered us doughboys to begin training from the day we arrived…daily drills, instruction in hand-to-hand combat, drills in bayonet fighting, gas training, trench warfare, and open combat. We have spent most days in the rain, wet and muddy. With dry socks, I sit and write to you, missing you, and wishing I was home with you and Moishie.

All my love,

Nicky

July 1, 1918

Dearest Miriam,

My unit has still not been called up to the front. The Germans began their Spring Offensive in March. Those few who have returned from the fighting–French, American, British–are a sight you'd never want to see. They are limbless, crippled, totally debilitated by mustard gas. We keep our spirits up after dinner at the mess hall each evening. Someone found an old piano, and we dragged it into the hall. Once the boys heard me play that old upright after dinner, they insisted that I play every night. The guys singalong as loud as they can. (There's no liquor here and that has become the biggest complaint.) The sergeant feels that singing is a good motivator, so he orders us to sing while we dig trenches with pickaxes and shovels, while we march, while we do calisthenics. Wouldn't you guess that there's a big river here? It's the Marne–and I talked to some buddies who have access to trucks and some French guys who own small vineyards around here. We'll see. They tell us we'll soon be deployed…a counteroffensive to the Boche Spring Offensive. We'll have to push toward the Champagne region, and the fighting will be fierce. But, as promised, I will be home in one piece as soon as this awful war ends. I am sure that Moishie is growing handsome and smart. Please give him a thousand hugs for me.

Love,

Nicky

July 6, 1918.

***

Miriam sat on a backyard blanket in the warmth of the summer sun with her four-month-old son. The letters kept coming but the more she read, the more frightened she grew. Natalya was of little help now. She was weak, fatigued, and spent much of the day in bed despite the warm sunny days. Things were different in other ways now. Miriam's mother, Rebecca Lewinsky, was now living with them and was a big help with the baby. Miriam's father died in France, another life experience she had to endure alone, without her Nicky. Losses, losses, and more losses. Frankly, she saw no end in sight. Of course, the American government would never allow the public to know the true death tolls, but between the lines, the journalists calculated Allied troop deaths in the millions, and over 100,000 Americans dead, and counting.

She feared how this was going to end. No matter what promises her Nicky made.

***

Dearest Miriam,

You'll never guess what happened. Yesterday, my friend Arnold Wotitsky came running into the barracks telling me that the captain wanted to see me immediately. Now I have to tell you, I was sure the captain was going to reprimand me, maybe even have me court-martialed. I hurried out of the bunk thinking what to say. As I told you, I had arranged a shipment of wine for the "dry" troops here but on the night of the planned delivery, the Krauts hit us with a three-hour bombing raid and the wine deal never took place. But you know how it is. People talk. There are no secrets. The entire camp is tense. Word is we're moving out any day to Chateau-Thierry for some big counter-offensive against the Germans near the Marne. The Germans are within 70 km. of Paris. No doubt their planes and artillery can reach the inner city. You know what's on everyone's mind. Am I going to come back? Of course, I am, I promise. Love to our beautiful baby boy. Love to you with all my heart. Please send my love to Natalya. The tide may be turning in this horrible war. I will write soon.

Love you always and forever,
Nicky
July 10, 1918

***

"Private Nikolai Stein reporting, sir."

"Do you know why you are here, Private?"

"I can explain, sir. It was a mistake, Captain. Nothing happened, sir."

"What are you babbling about, Private?"

"Sir, I just wanted to say…"

"I don't care what you want, Private."

"But…"

"Private. I have asked you here for a special assignment."

"Special assignment, sir?"

"Yes, Private. You are needed in Paris in 24 hours. I hear you're a darn good piano player."

"Well, sir, I…"

"Private, you will board the train to Paris at 0600 tomorrow. You will be escorted by two MPs. Upon your arrival in Paris, a car will be waiting to transport you to Montmartre. Folies Bergere to be exact. Seems that Major General Alphonse T. Huntington of the Third Infantry Division has insisted on going to the Folies Bergere tomorrow night. Turns out the regular piano player was recently killed in a bombing raid and his backup has influenza. Your name came up."

Chapter 26
Folies Bergere

The view for the first two hours of the train ride to Paris sickened Nikolai. The once beautiful summer countryside of France was pock-marked with deep trenches, huge mounds of erupting earth, craters big enough to swallow a house, once long emerald hedges and purple vineyards destroyed, and century-old majestic cypress trees felled in a moon-like landscape. The closer they got to Paris, the destruction lessened. He thought of his outfit, ordered and ready to move to the front today–sans Private Stein. Why was it that Nikolai Yakov Stein (nee' Schteinkov) from Odessa was chosen to go to Paris to play the piano? Why was he spared the fate of the rest of his comrades who were trudging off to rat-infested mud trenches, to bombs and artillery fire, strafing machine guns, and perhaps to gas-induced asphyxiation?

As the train pulled into Gare d'Austerlitz, he could see the bustling civilians, vendors, soldiers, and the battle-worn cripples going about their missions as if with blinders. Paris, he was told, had been largely spared in the past three years. The lines had held just short of the city. Yet now, with the Spring Offensive, the Boche were 70 miles outside Paris, close enough to reach with artillery and bombers.

Outfitted in his US Army dress uniform and flanked by two MPs, he stepped off the train and was escorted into a black Model A waiting outside the station. No words spoken. He hoped to glimpse the Arch de Triumph, or the Louvre, or at least the Eiffel Tower. But no—this was a military assignment. They sped off along the Seine via the Quai Saint Bernard with a loquacious French driver pointing out the sights: past the Jardins de Plantes, along the Quai de la Tournelle, past the Cathedrale Notre-Dame de Paris, across the Pont Neuf, over to Rue du Louvre past the Museum of the same name. The car sped up Rue du Faubourg-Montmartre and finally stopped on Rue Richer, overlooking Paris in the foothills of Montmartre.

Folies Bergere, opened in 1869, was now the premiere music hall in all of Paris. He was quickly led into the magnificent venue, passing the massive relief of shining gold ornamenting the entrance. As he entered the building, the central grand hall overwhelmed him with its shining dance floors, and walls of red, gold and ebony. A massive crystal chandelier led toward a cascading staircase. Large golden doors opened to a luxurious theater with red carpeting, gilded balconies, a huge stage, all crowned by an elaborately painted vaulted ceiling.

From behind a curtain, the theater manager, the music director, and the choreographer appeared. Neither looked him in the eyes…*Mon Dieu*, an American pianist at the Folies Bergere! For the next eight hours, Nikolai was crammed with the sheet music to song after song, act after act. How in the world would he pull this off? A dozen or so young girls lined up in their street clothes and the sets were being constructed. Rehearsal lasted right up until the time the curtain rose at 8 pm.

Men in tuxedos and women in lavish gowns sat at the cabaret tables, smoking or toying with drinks. This was Folies Bergere, after all, where the stage sets were exotic…gold and silver, flashing lights, and colors spanning the spectrum. Young, beautiful women danced in scanty costumes of sparse feathers and sparkling sequins, shiny boots and sparkling hats. Little else was left to the imagination. Young, lithe bodies wore G-strings decorated with any fruit of your choice.

But tonight, the American major general was in the house. Private Nikolai Stein played American favorites like "Yankee Doodle Dandy" and "The Star-Spangled Banner" while the chorus danced in scanty bits of stars and stripes, as parts of the American flag streamed from the trapeze high above. A taut woman about 18 was perched on high with three stars strategically placed on her body.

Everyone ignored the rumbling of bombs and artillery. Of course, the show must go on. The building trembled. but those who were drinking and laughing and oohing and aahing barely noticed. Paris had escaped significant damage or destruction, so as the thunderous noises erupted, neither the audience nor the entertainers gave it much thought. The drone of the shelling was imperceptible at first. If anyone at the musical revue heard it at all, the booming sounds would have appeared far off. When there was a pause in the show, the whirling of shells grew louder. And the louder the bombing got, the louder Nikolai and his band played.

An army of semi-clad dancers herded onto the stage as the can-can finale began. The music and the singing reached a feverish pitch. The shrieks of the artillery shells could still be heard…shrieks to and from nowhere.

Suddenly, an explosion. A shell penetrated the roof and landed on stage. Bodies and fragments flew. People took cover. There was nowhere to hide. Shell after shell landed on one side of the hall, then the other. All around now. The lights failed. The screaming reached a crescendo. Nikolai inhaled the pungent odor of the smoke and dirt, the iron aroma of blood. Crashing and burning and yelling and then…nothing.

Chapter 27
Home Again

"We're so glad you're home, Nicky," said Miriam as she sat in the kitchen nursing their son Moishie. "Having you here these last several months while you've been recovering has been a dream come true. Moishie knows you now. He follows your every move."

"We're so happy that you didn't get yourself killed in that stupid war, like your uncle did for that crazy Kaiser," said Natalya. She bent over her coffee, trembling some as she brought the cup to her lips.

"I know I asked you a million times, sweetheart, but I just can't believe it. I keep thinkin' about it. So your commanding officer orders you to play at that place with all the naked girls, the bombs came, and the piano fell on you? You're lucky it was only a broken leg and your losing the last two fingers on your left hand. You could have lost a leg, or a whole hand, or worse. Good thing your soldier buddies pulled you out of that mess and got you to the American hospital."

"Better a month in the hospital then home, than a month at the front and home in a box. Poor bastards. You should have seen that place…bombed to hell. Right at the can-can finale too," said the young US Army physician at the hospital in Paris.

Nikolai stared at his son and smiled. *My father's eyes and my wife's complexion,* thought Nikolai. Nikolai could not contain his sense of pride and joy of seeing Miriam again, laying eyes on Moishie for the first time, the comfort of seeing Natalya. He balanced that joy with the gravity of the support that he now had to provide, the responsibility he had to shoulder. Pressure to be sure. In fact, it all seemed quite intimidating. He loved this woman and, of course, his first-born son, with a full heart he never quite knew. From a whirlwind of running away, to the dangers and sights and sounds of war, to the escape somehow from the horrors of mortal combat, he now stood on an unsteady leg and outstretched hands that would never play another note. What to do?

***

"Nicky doesn't know what to do," Miriam cried to Natalya. "He says he loves me and Moishie more than anything. But I get that feeling like he thinks he's supposed to. I don't get that *tears-in-the-eyes feeling* from him. Oh, maybe for brief moments here and there."

"He tells me he can't stop thinking about the last few months," said Natalya in a weak voice. "Ever since those shots rang out in the music store…deserting his family, running from the law, the military, being far off overseas, coming home with a limp and two finger stubs, and a lost chance to ever play his music again."

"Well, private, looks like you lucked out," said the tall young army doctor with dark circles below his eyes. "Over a hundred people died in that bombing raid, and we're not finished counting. Lot of pretty girls hurt to boot. Direct hit. Lucky for you that big old piano fell on you. Protected you from some of the fire and brimstone. Nothing too serious. Nothing life-changing. Just a broken femur and a couple of missing fingers. You're going home, soldier. That's the end of the war for you."

Miriam and Nicky spent the rest of the year catching up with each other, caring for their beautiful son, monitoring Miriam's pregnancy, but also watching the slow but sure dwindling of Natalya's strength. Natalya died quietly one evening in her sleep. She was given a proper burial. As Nikolai stood at the gravesite, images of the past fluttered by…walks on the Black Sea shore with his parents—the strong eyes of his father, Moyshe-Yakov, and the warm smile of his mother, Esther; the journey to America with Natalya; the freedom of playing the piano to his heart's content for Mr. Rosenberg.

***

"These picnics are my favorite times," said Nicky. Miriam spread out the blanket in the park and made a place for Moishie to sit down.

She sat awkwardly, moving slowly in her ninth month of pregnancy. It was 1921. Nicky had been home over two years now and was back working for King Solomon. Miriam was back singing at the club. Prohibition was in full swing, and business was booming. And another on the way. Yet, somehow, it wasn't enough. Or maybe it was too much.

"Me too, but I worry about your working for Charles again."

"Yeah, and I'm always looking over my shoulder. What else can I do? I can't play anymore. It's the only way I know how to make money. I'm no further ahead than I was before I left for that stinkin' France."

"Maybe he'll give you a promotion or somethin'. Somethin' a little less risky."

"Truth is, the Italians are moving in. The Irish are out for blood. Vicious competition. Things are more complicated for Charlie now. Somethin's got to change."

"Change? Nicky, we're just getting settled again. Moishie's growing fast, and I'm due in a few weeks."

"Yeah, I'm going to talk to Solomon about that."

Chapter 28
A Sudden Departure

"Congratulations, Nick! A cute baby girl. A May baby. Now that you've been back with the gang for a few years, money in your pocket again, booze flowing like the Mississippi, you're sittin' pretty. What's her name?" asked Billy, Nick's co-worker. The two waited in the dark for the liquor shipment to be loaded onto trucks at Swampscott Harbor off Nahant Bay on a moonless night.

"Gloria Esther. She's cute alright, and another mouth to feed. It's lucky we have Miriam's mother helping out every once in a while. Since France, I've done nothing but look over my shoulder. Cops, FBI, our Italian and Irish friends in the neighborhood. Tell you the truth, I don't feel so good. Charlie says I'm a risk. What he calls a liability. He's been talking about my joining up with a friend of his. Some guy named Bernstein in Detroit. A bunch called The Purple Gang."

"If that's going to make you feel better? Not so trapped. Not so nervous. Not feeling like you're under their watch all the time," said Billy.

"Yeah, well, I just can't do it. I can't play the piano anymore. That kept me grounded. Happy. But that's all water under the bridge. I'd be leaving my wife and kids, but only for a short time. Sure, I'll wire them money. But I'm not sure I'm cut out to do this husband/father thing. It may be time to vacate for a while," said Nick.

"Yeah, well, you gotta' do what you gotta' do. Look, I gotta' go. The shipment's all loaded. You'll figure it out," said Billy. "I'll have these guys drive the load up to Manchester tonight. See you in a couple of days."

"Yeah. Good luck. I'll see you."

***

"Like I said, son, it's getting real dangerous around here," said King Solomon. "Yeah, it's 1922, and the liquor is flowing like Niagara Falls. The clubs are busier than ever. Too bad this ain't going to last forever.

But for you, the word's been out on the street for a while that you're back, fingers or no fingers. Eyes are watching."

"I know. I can feel heat. Breathing down my neck. I hear things."

"Yeah, things are being said, alright. Things are rough enough in our racket. I'm down a half-dozen guys since New Year's, if you know what I mean. It's specially not safe for you. The Feds still have their knickers in a twist over what happened in that music store."

"Yeah, things come back to bite you in the ass, I guess."

"Listen, there are no promotions, no more territories to divide. I know you got that wife and those two kids, but it might have been safer for you over in that shithole in France than it is for you here."

"So what am I supposed to do, Boss?"

"Listen up. A colleague of mine, guy named Abe Bernstein's looking for a few good guys like you. Him and his brothers started even before me. They moved from New York City to Detroit. A bunch of badass boys took advantage of the Midwest business, across the river from Canada. They've done well for themselves. Made nice to Capone in Chicago. He leaves them alone, and they leave him alone. Go to Detroit for a while. Make good there and then come back. It is still too hot here for you. You know what I mean."

"You think that's what I should do? You can arrange that?"

"I'll fix you up. Grease the skids. He's a Yid like us. The whole bunch of 'em are Yids. They got a good thing going. They're on the border with Canada, where booze is still legal there. Trust me."

"What about my wife and kids? What will happen to them?"

"Don't worry. I'll see to them. They're in Newton now, right? They'll be OK. You'll come and visit now and then."

"Charlie, you don't get it. I was never happier in my life than when I was playing the piano. Anytime. Anywhere. And man, when I was playing for you at the club, playing for Miriam...that was paradise. Heaven. Now what do I do? A wife. Couple of kids to support. And guys at both ends squeezing to cut off the rest of my fingers."

"Better visits than no old man at all. I'm tellin' you."

***

"Oh, come on, Nicky. It's our fourth anniversary. It's been so nice. You taking me out to the Lamb's Club, bringing me flowers, buying me this beautiful dress."

"Anything for you. It sure seems like you liked your food. You cleaned your plate and some of mine. By the way, I heard you in the bathroom this morning, throwing up. And you have seemed really tired lately. You OK?"

"Oh, Nicky, I hope you don't ever have to go away again. What would I do? What would the kids do?"

"Listen, I've survived this long. Cops breathing down my neck. All I know is that we are going to keep Moishie in that music school. I wanted him to play the piano, but it seems like he's taken to the trumpet. He sounds real good. A Satchmo prodigy. And Gloria. She's going to be a singer like her mother and her Grandmother Esther in the old country. I can tell already. And a dancer. So raise that glass of champagne of yours and let's toast to us and the kids. And let's have that dance you promised me."

***

As Nikolai washed his hands in the men's room at the Lamb's Club that evening, he heard the door open and close. He now stood at the sink with something hard and cold against his right temple. Nikolai froze. He raised his hands. He couldn't see the guy behind him but he smelled of cigarettes and alcohol.

"No sudden moves. You're coming with me. I wouldn't try any funny stuff if you know what's good for you. Nice and quiet. We're just going to walk out of here together, out through the kitchen, and out the back door." *No fucking way,* thought Nick. *On our anniversary?*

As the two moved slowly out the back door and into the calm summer evening, Nikolai could only think of those God-awful, good-for-nothing training drills that he and the other recruits suffered through in boot camp, waiting to go to the Western Front.

"Just keep movin' pal." Suddenly, Nick kicked back with his right leg. He turned and swung his left elbow hard into his attacker's jaw. Instinctively he brought his left leg around and kicked his assailant in the groin. As The Suit bent forward, Nick delivered a stiff uppercut to the Adam's apple with his right hand. The revolver went flying. As the figure before him groaned and crumpled to the ground, Nikolai ran. And he ran and ran and ran…to nowhere. He had to go. Now.

Chapter 29
The Purple Gang

"So you're the new guy Charlie sent over from Boston?" said Abraham Bernstein.

"That's right," said Nikolai, sitting in front of the leader of Detroit's Purple Gang.

"How was the train ride? Must have been long and dry."

"Both," quipped Nikolai.

Abe took out a large bottle of Canadian Club from his dilapidated desk drawer. Stogie between his fat lips, he placed it on the desktop with a thud. Two murky whiskey glasses appeared from another drawer. Bernstein poured the glasses to the brim. He pushed one of the glasses toward Nikolai and raised the other in his right hand.

"*L'Chaim.* Drink up. Don't get better than this. Straight from Hiram Walker."

"*L'Chaim.*"

"Welcome to our outfit. I told Charlie that I could use a guy like you. A guy that knows the business, experienced, smart, another Yid. Too bad it got too hot for you in Boston."

Nikolai sat, and swigged and listened to his new boss talk about The Purple Gang. Bernstein was a large, heavy-set man, with wavy dark hair, deep dark eyes, big hairy ears, large nose that appeared to veer to the right, and a dark mole on his right cheek. He wore a schlumpy brown double-breasted suit with his tie at half-mast. He leaned back in an old wooden chair behind the desk. The office was sparse. No pictures, no books, dark walls and a thin grey carpet with no design. A black phone sat on the desk. A small radio sat on the lone shelf behind him. The place reeked of cigar smoke, whose source was a large glass ashtray, filled to the brim with butts, resting in the center of the old oak desk.

"So as I was saying, you probably know, we're all Jews. Families from the old country. Better that way. Helps with the trust factor. Detroit: We own this town. Me and my brothers started before anybody…1917. Even before Prohibition. Speakeasies, casinos, every liquor shipment from

Canada across the river, laundries, whorehouses. There's not a part of anything in this town that the Purple Gang doesn't get a piece of. No matter what that Jew-hater Henry Ford thinks. He can go fuck himself."

"You, I'm putting you in charge of the shipments coming across from Canada. We get most of our booze through Windsor, Ontario, across the river. Some of it comes from my good friend Bronfman. Another smart Jew. You won't have any trouble with the law. We've got that handled. But you may need a few of my muscle guys around you... with Tommy guns, of course. I got you a flat at the Collingwood Manor for now. You married? Kids?"

"Yes, Mr. Bernstein. A wife, a boy and a girl, outside Boston. But they'll be remaining there for now."

"Good. I need you to get to work. No distractions. You know what I mean, boychik?"

"Yes, sir."

"Keep your nose clean, kid. You'll do alright."

***

Months flew by. The bootlegging operation was no simple business. It was far from a slick and easy operation for the Purple Gang. They were constantly on alert for attacks on their truckloads of booze, never sparing any brutality in defense of their payload. Anti-Semitism played no small role in the ebbs and flows of the lucrative enterprise of providing liquor to thirsty Americans.

And yet, the Jews moved liquor like ants building their hills. Boatloads, truckloads. And try to stop them? God help anyone who tried. They owned Detroit. The Purple Gang was as vicious and brutal as any criminal mob in the country. Barring none. Word was "the big man from Chicago," Al Capone, would not venture into Detroit. He did not want to risk more bloodshed. He spilled enough of his own.

The Bernstein brothers (Abraham, Raymond, Isadore, and Joseph) liked the way Nikolai managed the buying, transporting, and distribution of their product. Because of his mangled hand, among other things, the bosses rarely asked Nikolai to get involved in their other rackets…extortion, gambling, hijackings, revenge murders. They kept him out of gun battles and most of the physical end of the business. Nikolai was aware over the years of guys dropping like flies. From 1927 to 1933, many of the highest-ranking members of the Purple Gang, known for their savagery, were sent to prison for life. They staged hundreds of murders, not the least of which included the Milaflores and Collingwood Manor Massacres. In September 1931, The Purple Gang committed the vicious murders of three Chicago hoodlums who betrayed the members of the Detroit gang. These gangland slayings made the front page of every paper in the country. By some estimates, over 500 thugs were sent to their graves at the hands of the Purple Gang during their reign.

Every gang member was either born in "the old country" or born to parents who fled from the pogroms of the nineteenth century, particularly in Russia. These massacres were perpetrated by a mob mentality that included police officers, soldiers, and townspeople. Violence for the sake of violence. These senseless murders seemed to fulfill that instinctive urge for sheer brutality, brought down upon scapegoated persons, that was approved, condoned, and rewarded by the powers that be. Was this the other side of the coin? Was the brutality of the Purple Gang any different from the latter scenario? Generational revenge and pent-up anger?

By 1928, Nick was known less as an enforcer than as a wizard with organizational skills and talents for creative problem solving. He managed crews of men who moved product across the Canadian border "come rain, or sleet, or snow, or the FBI." He became a can-do guy, no matter what the circumstances. More brains than brawn. He stood solid physically, trained by the US Army at the prime of his life…strong, imposing, handsome, but thoughtful, imaginative, even conniving.

***

Nikolai kept to himself. His phone calls home grew less frequent. His family received fewer and fewer envelopes of cash. The tether was beginning to unravel. Then the call came.

"I know it's kinda dangerous but you gotta come home. Our little girl, Gloria, is really sick. They say she has polio."

"Polio? Jesus Christ. But she's only eight years old."

"Nicky, please come home. I'm begging you. I thought at first it was the flu. But she got worse and worse." A stab in the heart. A wake-up call. His family.

"Is she home? Has she seen a doctor?"

"Nicky, it's real bad. She can't breathe. She's in the hospital. She's on one of those iron lungs." A pulling…toward his child, his wife, his boy.

Chapter 30
Home Again

Nikolai sat by his daughter's bedside. The bird in the bed was pale, listless, mute, bedsheets up to her chin. Miriam sat red-eyed, wringing her hands, intermittent outbursts of crying. Moishie, now a teenager…taller, neatly dressed, staring out the hospital window. The family was together again.

Moishie's father had been away in Detroit from 1923 to 1930. The visits, the phone calls, the letters had dwindled to once or twice a year on holidays. He once idolized his father. The boy lived fatherless the last many years with his mother and sister and maternal grandmother, Rebecca Lewinsky. He kept to himself a lot. Grade school and junior high were boring to him. What was not boring to him was his music. Miriam had enrolled him in the Berklee College of Music Junior Program at the age of eight. While Miriam, and his teachers, and staff members tried to coerce Moishie into playing the piano or violin (at which he excelled in his own right), it was the trumpet that felt right to him.

The pages of the world were turning. The Roaring Twenties and Prohibition rolled in with its free-flowing bootlegged liquor and speakeasies. Jazz was king. And then 1929…The Great Depression blanketed the nation. "Buddy, can you spare a dime?" But the music continued, and the radio herded the world together. From an early age, Moishie would work on his embouchure, day and night to produce a clean, resonant tone. He'd listen for hours to the greats on the radio, the likes of Doc Cheatham, Bix Beiderbecke, Jabba Smith, Louis Panico, Hot Lips Page, Cootie Williams, and, of course. Louie Armstrong and Dizzy Gillespie.

But what was a growing young man supposed to do without a father at home? A father to encourage forward motion; to help rein in that growing strength; someone to see that burgeoning passion exuding from every pore knowing it required channeling; a father to model right from wrong, reality from fantasy, someone to explain the difference between strength and brutishness. And so, should Moishie have felt guilty about sneaking off after school, or even during school via the MBTA to this club or that club? Into the bowels of Boston or surrounding towns to watch the jazz boats jam while his sister was so sick? He yearned to pick up some pointers, adopt a style or two, while his mother visited Gloria in the hospital. With no father to take the family helm, he was a teenager, unknowingly searching for some direction, holding on to a rudder by himself, no one to either guide him nor to relieve him as he tried to steer a steady course.

***

One week later, Gloria was dead.

"Nothing more we could do. I'm sorry," said the doctor.

The funeral was small, a local cemetery on the outskirts of Newton. Few words were spoken. Miriam tried to take solace, with mixed emotions, from her husband. He'd been away. He'd stopped coming home to see her, to see his son and daughter. And the letters, the money, had petered. Two children to care for. She hadn't seen him. The kids had not seen him for over two years.

Moishie spent as much time as he could, sitting and talking to Nikolai. The boy pummeled his father about his work, his gang, and Detroit music.

"You're what? You're working for who?" cried Nikolai.

"King Charles treats me well. I'm Nikolai's son after all. We need the money, Papa. Mom's out of money. We had hospital bills. We couldn't pay for my music lessons anymore. It's just small errands. It lets me see the best trumpeters, local musicians and visiting bands. I learn a lot, and occasionally they let me practice with them."

"That's unacceptable. I don't want you working for him," cried Nikolai.

"And Mom's back singing at his clubs. I thought you knew."

"It's not right. It's no good. Look what it did to me. To us. You wait. I will come home sooner than you think." And with that, Nikolai left Miriam and Moishie again, this time intending to return home, no matter what the cost. He would talk to his boss, Abe Bernstein. As he stared out the window of the train back to Detroit, he was determined, and convinced at least for the moment, that the Steins of Newton needed to be a family again. He had lost his son once. More than once. He'd lost his daughter forever. He wouldn't do it again.

***

And just like that, his father left him again, as Moishe tried to remember the longest stint that his father had spent with him, telling him stories of his birthright, sharing nuances about their mutual passion for music. But this time, his father promised he would come home soon. He promised…as his mother had promised that time she left him. He was a toddler, maybe two or three. His father had not visited home in six to eight months.

"Mommy will come home soon. In a couple of months. I promise. Bubbie Lewinsky will take good care of you. I'll be home in no time."

"But where are you going, Mommy?"

"Mommy just has to go away for a while, Moishie."

And she did come home… in two months, an eternity. A little paler, more tearful. Moishie remembers the tears. She rained hugs and kisses on her boy like never before.

Chapter 31
A Mench

"Sidney, I just don't know what to do," complained Lenore Lavovsky to her husband.

"Lee, we've been over this a million times. When the time is right, we'll tell him."

"For God's sakes. We're not in the old country anymore. It's the mid 1930s. He's been bar mitzvahed and confirmed. He'll soon be going off to college. He's always been such a *mench*. Always did what we asked of him. Worked in the store since he was a boy. He deserves to know."

"I know. I know. I just don't want to break his heart. Maybe next week."

"Sid, we've said that since he could talk. First grade. Second grade. Junior high. Where did the time go? And now he says he wants to be a doctor. Do you think it is right for a doctor not to know that he's adopted?"

"No. You're right. We could not have kept the grocery going without his help all these years. Such a good boy. We'll tell him next week," Sidney said. He turned the key to lock the little shop on Union Street in Lynn, Massachusetts.

***

Israel Lavovsky sat down to study for his first Neurology exam during his third year at Harvard Medical School. He learned about seizure disorders--Jacob-Creutzfeldt disorder, Gillian-Barre Syndrome, the Gate Control Theory of Pain, Parkinson's Disease, Motor Neuron diseases, especially a rare but increasingly diagnosed affliction, mostly in children…Poliomyelitis. The field was wide open, and it excited him. His book remained closed as he mused about a sea change that occurred in his life several years ago. Weeks before he left for college, he was practicing his violin in his bedroom, Brahms Violin Concerto in D Major. His parents were surprised when he turned down a scholarship to

Berklee College of Music to accept a chance to go to Harvard University. His undergraduate classes in biology and chemistry furthered his focus from music to pre-med. When he was accepted to Harvard Medical School, his excitement could not be understated. What a time to be studying medicine with research and new ideas opening the way to discoveries like antibiotics, vaccines, x-rays, new techniques of surgery, anesthesia, radiation and biochemistry.

There was a knock at the bedroom door. It surprised him. His parents never interrupted his violin practice. He stopped playing, rose to his feet, and opened the door. His parents stood there with sheepish grins, asked in unison, "Can we come in? We want to talk to you about something."

"Are you OK? Did something happen? You look scared."

"No. Nothing happened," they said together, shaking their heads at each other, as his mother sat on the edge of his bed and his father walked over to stand next to her.

"Then what's up?"

"Well…" said Lenore, pausing interminably as she looked up at Sidney.

"You know, Izzie," said Sidney. Israel noticed his father trembling.

"Your mother and I were immigrants from czarist Russia, well actually Ukraine. And we came to this country with plans to live a free life and raise a family," he said, looking down at Lenore.

"We tried, everything, but were unable to have children…And there was this agency, Louise Wise Agency, the only adoption agency for Jewish families and so…"

Shock.

Israel took it better than they thought he would. He hadn't questioned much. These were his parents after all. They were all he knew. He was an only child. They had been nothing but kind and loving and supportive. He had at times some vague signals from the core of his emotional quotient, like one of the family jokes as to why neither Sidney nor Lenore had one amino acid of musical talent going back generations.

"So do you know anything about my biological parents?"

"Well…no. It was against the rules. The agency lady did slip-up once and said your mother was a singer and your father was some kind of musician."

True, as he examined himself in the mirror as all teenagers do, the image of a handsome, well-conditioned youth with soft black hair and blue eyes caused a tickle of doubt. He thought of his father, who was tall and lanky with brown eyes and a dark brown horseshoe of hair around his bald head. His mother was blonde, buxom, and heavy.

He never tried to find out who his birth parents were. He thought that such a search might hurt them deeply. Not that he didn't wonder who was out there. A nagging thought. A constant on and off question that niggled at his inquisitive mind. But it was not the time to scratch at this itch. His parents had brought him up to be honest, hard-working, forthright, and to mind his own business. At the dinner table each night the lesson/instruction was clear: Never forget your sense of "familial security."

"Izzie, remember, you will always be a Jew." Left unsaid was, *"You will always be seen by others as a Jew…different, an outsider, not fitting in. But never forget your heritage. And family. The most important. Your family will always be there for you and you will always be there for your family."*

But, for now, his eyes were on the prize—to be a first-rate neurologist. He had dragons to slay. Discipline. Study. Knowledge. Important discoveries to make. He was going to get his medical degree and cure the world. He was going to be the hardest working, the most honorable, the brightest doctor ever.

Chapter 32
An Untimely Death

Nikolai planned to meet with his boss Abe Bernstein. The global winds were shifting. FDR was now president. Hitler was now in power, and the Germans were arming again. Prohibition had been repealed. Stalin was busy with dekulakization, starving and killing his own Russian people, as the Bolshevik/Jewish conspiracy theories raced through Europe. The Great Depression was smothering much of the world like an intergalactic wet blanket. The New Deal was kicking in and the bootleggers' days of glory were waning. The Detroit Machine was imploding. The major Purple Gang leaders were either dead, or indicted and behind bars.

Abe Bernstein called Nick into his office. An assignment. A request that Nikolai would never have imagined.

"Look, we can all feel it. Business is slow. The heat is turning up. The noose is getting tighter. You've done a good job. You need to leave before they put the squeeze on you like the rest of us. I'm particularly talking to you because a brother has a request of you. This one, you don't say no to. He's at the top. Nobody bigger. I recommended you."

"Thanks, Mr. Bernstein. That means a lot."

"I assume you've heard of…", at this point Bernstein leaned over and whispered something in Nikolai's ear. Abe realized recently that the walls of his office were thinner than he thought.

Nikolai had, of course, heard of Mr. L. Who hadn't? One of the most infamous criminals in the US, perhaps the richest. Said to be worth $20 million (equivalent to $184,000,000 today). A Jewish mobster who started in New York City but eventually controlled gambling, liquor distribution, and night clubs in New York, Miami, New Orleans, and Cuba. He financed operations in London, the Bahamas, and Nevada.

"He wants to meet with you. He also wants to meet with your son and wife. Take off. Go back to Boston and your family. Don't worry. The heat's off in Beantown. The law won't bother you. We took care of that."

"Well, I'm not sure I'll miss this place, being away from my family and all. But it's been nice knowing you, Boss."

"Well, you take care of yourself, boychik. Mr. L's men will be in touch. And by the way, I guess you heard the news."

Berstein handed Nick the newspaper.

BOSTON, Jan. 24, 1933

SYNDICATE LEADER GUNNED DOWN IN DOWNTOWN NIGHTCLUB

Charles (King) Solomon, reputed leader of the most lucrative liquor, vice and narcotic syndicates in New England and proprietor of several nightclubs, was shot while he was in the wash-room of the Cotton Club in Roxbury, early this morning and died at City Hospital several hours later, cursing "those dirty rats" who shot him.

"Too bad for Charlie. He had a good run. May God rest his soul," said Abe.

Chapter 33
An Order from the Top

Israel Lavovsky skipped a grade in junior high and high school and graduated early. Despite the Jewish quotas, Izzie was accepted to the Harvard University Pre-med Program. His family could not afford a college education, let alone a medical school tuition. He joined Navy ROTC as an undergraduate. He kept to himself, absorbed in his studies. He was a model student. He had little social life. He lived at home and continued to help his parents in the store. He was a dutiful son, supporting his parents in any way he could. Whatever issues or questions arose at home, the answer was always, *Family is everything.* If he had a fight with his parents, the verbal war would undoubtedly end with, *Look, family is everything. Zy gazunt (Enough. That's all).* If they discussed his leaving home, attending holiday dinners, fights about the family dog, the final word was always, *Family matters.* Studying through the summers, he finished his pre-med work in three years. Nothing but accolades and awards followed in his wake. He even merited the musician of the year award, concluding his final semester by playing Mozart's Adelaide, his Violin Concerto No. 8 at Boston's Symphony Hall.

Medical school and his neurology residency went smoothly, with words of praise coming from his colleagues and teachers alike. A professor said of him, "He is a young physician who thinks far beyond his years of education and experience." Another said, "Kind, empathic, patient, honest to a fault, calming, appropriate sense of humor, excellent personal values, of the highest integrity." He was accepted as an attending physician at the National Institute of Neurological Disorders and Stroke, in Bethesda, Maryland and became the youngest faculty member of Georgetown Medical School, in Washington, DC. His passion blossomed.at the National Institute of Health where he practiced in the complicated world of neurological diseases, an unending list of devastating conditions with no effective treatments, no cures, and even less understanding as to their etiology.

It was at this juncture that a knock came to his door at 6 am one morning at his studio apartment in Washington, DC. He opened the door.

"Ensign Israel Lavovsky?" asked one of the two lieutenant commanders in US Navy full dress standing at Izzie's threshold.

"Yes sir," saluted Dr. Israel Lavovsky in his pajamas.

"Get dressed, ensign. You have been ordered to come with us immediately."

"But where to? I have laboratory work to do, hospital assignments that I must attend to, patients to see."

"We have been asked to escort you to National Naval Medical Center in Bethesda."

"Bethesda Naval Hospital? What? Why?"

"Dr. Lavovsky, the President of the United States of America has asked to see you."

PART IV

Chapter 34
A Family Offer Not to be Refused

Nikolai tried to start his own legitimate liquor store business, but after getting held up three times at gunpoint, he found a position as a table games floor supervisor at one of the Boston casinos. Miriam grabbed any singing gig she could muster. Moishie scratched out the occasional trumpet gig. He found a few short-term jobs giving trumpet lessons. He was fortunate to find himself, because of his virtuosity, at the top of the lists of many of the local musical talent agents. The booking agent for the Boston Symphony Orchestra and Tanglewood threw him a bone or two occasionally. Things were tough for most families in the US and the Stein family was no exception.

A young, talented man stuck in the arms of the Great Depression. Money, jobs, and even a place to live were difficult to find for most. Congress repealed the Volstead Act. Illegal bootlegging graduated to lawful liquor sales, and in some cases, "legal" casino gambling gave birth to so-called carpet joints. Bolshevism, fascism, and communism were all taking shape and were raging not only in Asia and Europe but were infiltrating American society. International Axis alliances formed and a militaristic Germany and Japan were surreptitiously preparing for regional, if not world dominance.

At least they were a family again, thought Moishie, watching his father drink a cold beer on a warm Sunday afternoon in the summer of 1936. Moishie, Miriam, and Nikolai, sat by the radio, listening to the all-too-familiar score by Rossini, the William Tell Overture, as the Lone Ranger Radio Hour began. He couldn't remember when the three of them had been together, relaxed. The word "relaxed" had fallen out of the American vocabulary in those angry days of the mid-thirties. As the decade unfolded, eyes and hearts and souls of Americans were being drawn toward brutal divides. Chasms opened up. Battles raged between haves and have-nots, between various ethnic, religious and cultural interests: Ku Klux Klan, German Nazi sympathizers (the German American Bund), Communists, and a meteoric rise in antisemitism. National pride in America's most celebrated hero, Charles Lindbergh, suffered a devastating blow when news arose of the flying ace's support for Nazi Germany.

FDR's New Deals helped, but not enough. True, there were superhuman WPA projects ignited by FDR's enthusiastic stewardship…Empire State Building, Hoover Dam, Tennessee Valley Authority followed soon thereafter by the secretive Oak Ridge facility. But most got a job when and where and if they could.

As the Steins listened to the Lone Ranger radio broadcast, the telephone rang.

"Mr. L. wants to see you," said a deep, Lower East Side New York City accent. The phone call Abe Bernstein had predicted.

"Mr. L.? When? Who is this? Now?"

"Now," came the curt voice.

"Where do I go? How do I get there?"

"We will deliver three train tickets to you."

"Tickets to where?"

"Boston to Miami."

"Why three?"

"Mr. L. wants to see you, your wife, and your son."

"What? He wants to see my whole family?"

"That's what I said, buster. You'll get an envelope that will take care of all your expenses. When you and your family arrive in Miami in five days, someone will pick you up at the train station. We've arranged a place for you to stay. You'll be starting work for Mr. L. next week."

"And what if we decide that it wouldn't be a good idea to…."

"Oh, I wouldn't do that if I were you or your wife or your son. If you know what's good for you, you'll be on that train. You'll be paid more than you ever hoped for. See you in five days." Click.

***

"So are we all agreed? We will be headed for Miami tomorrow," said Nikolai.

"Not much choice. It will be an adventure. An opportunity. Certainly a chance to get out of all this ice and snow," said Moishie.

"Looks like it will be a second chance for all of us. I just wish my daughter and son were coming with us," said Miriam, looking down in her lap.

"What? What are you saying, Mom? I'm coming. Me, your son is going with you. What are you talking about? I wish Gloria was alive and coming with us too." Moishie's eyes grew moist as he looked down at the floor.

"I'm not sure what you are saying, Miriam. I knew leaving Boston would bring up sad and confusing memories," said Nikolai. The father, the husband, full of hopes and dreams.

"But this is a new beginning. A fresh start. A chance for all of us to rise above this rotten, demoralizing Depression."

***

It was the mid-1930s. Automobiles were being mass produced…Fords, Chevrolets, Chryslers; sedans and trucks of all types. Sixty percent of US households had radios, and telephones were no longer a super luxury. The violent bootlegging and racketeering as a result of Prohibition had morphed into more sophisticated, and less murderous organizations of illegal gambling. Casinos and dinner/nightclubs, so-called carpet joints mushroomed. Jazz artists starred in the big cities…New York, Chicago, Detroit, Los Angeles, New Orleans, Las Vegas, Miami. But the country's biggest rage were the Big Bands…Tommy Dorsey, Glenn Miller, Louis Armstrong, Gene Cooper, Duke Ellington, Count Basie, Harry Roy and his Orchestra. Meanwhile, via the tabloids, FBI, union newsletters, and investigative journalism, the public learned about Organized Crime.

***

"How are your accommodations?"

"The apartment is beautiful, Mr. L," said Miriam.

"Look," said Mr. L. sitting across from the Steins, on his lanai in Miami, taking a drag on his cigarette. He wasn't fancy. In fact, he looked kind of schlumpy...early 60's, whitish hair in disarray, skinny, bulbous nose and sagging jowls. He sported a short sleeve cotton button down beach shirt unbuttoned at the top revealing wisps of grey chest hair, wrinkled and baggy linen pants with leather sandals that revealed his manicured toe nails.

"Now that you're settled in, here's the deal," said Mr. L. deeply inhaling his Camel cigarette and exhaling through his nose. "I control several casinos in Broward County. Casinos that are part of dinner clubs and nightclubs. We run mostly in the winter and bring the Northern crowd down here. Just to let you know, we run several joints in Saratoga Springs, New York, in the summer. Same deal. Now I can bring croupiers, chefs, waiters, waitresses and bar men and women back and forth. But you are my people. I know all about you. I need you, Nikolai, to manage the liquor end of things. I've heard good things about your musical talents as well as your ability to handle merchandise"

"Thank you, sir. I'm sure I can handle the job."

"You, Miriam, will handle recruiting, hiring, and firing of singers and dancers and comic talent."

"Wow. Thank you, Mr. L. I already made lists of talents and agents to call."

"And Moishie, I heard you play a mean horn. I am going to have you handle all the musicians: big bands, smaller bands, soloists. All legit. All above board. I spare no expense in hiring the best entertainment, the best food at our dinner clubs, the best of everything. I run a smooth operation. Efficient. No mistakes. I am hiring the whole Stein crew because I trust you. Of course, I have my ways. I know of your parents, grandparents, where you were born, where your families are from. Like me. The old country. You will be involved with many high-end establishments in Florida and Saratoga.

"Are those the only two locations we'll be working, Mr. L?"

"As a matter of fact, we're working on several hotels and casinos with my friend Colonel Batista in Cuba. In time, you may hear about the Bahamas, London, New Orleans, and Las Vegas. You will be treated fairly, have a home provided to you, and will be paid handsomely. Got it?"

"Yes, sir," they answered in unison.

"One more thing," smiled the gangster with a cigarette hanging from his lips. "Keep your eyes and ears open and your mouths shut. If you do that, we'll all get along fine."

The Steins sat up straight, looked at each other, wide-eyed, and tight lipped.

"Sure thing, Mr. L.," Nikolai finally said. He had not smiled as brightly in a very long time."

***

And so the Stein family, wounded but together, settled in the heart of a burgeoning tourist industry, into a new culture wrapped in South American influences, of shady real estate profiteers, of New York high rollers evading the cold winters and ready to deliver their money into the hands of the pre-war syndicate, whose name few dared to whisper: The Mafia. Mr. L., unflashy, unobtrusive, behind the scenes, controlled the entire operation from the Canadian border to the tip of Florida, 90 miles from Havana.

Chapter 35
An Unexpected Assignment

Lieutenant Commander Israel Lavovsky sat at his desk in the small room on the first floor of the Hyde Park home of the President of the United States. He was finishing his notes, recording his findings from the interview and physical exam of his renowned patient.

As usual, Izzy took the commercial train up. The presidential train took a separate and somewhat parallel track, from Washington, DC, to Baltimore to New York City, up the Hudson Valley past Poughkeepsie, finally stopping at Hyde Park, New York. He stared out the window of the mansion at the expansive gardens and deep woods to the east that hid the mighty Hudson. Private train tracks rose above the banks just behind The Big House.

***

Through his office telescope, the president watched the many boats sailing up the river to Albany and down river toward New York harbor. FDR was no stranger to sailing. He sailed down the Hudson as a young boy with his father, up the New England coast to Campobello, the family island summer retreat; sailing as a teenager his own sloop, *Half Moon,* around the islands of New Brunswick. Years later, he would be appointed Assistant Secretary of the Navy in 1931 by President Woodrow Wilson. But ten years earlier, despite his passion for the sea, he stopped sailing. His ability to sail the open seas, to haul the mainsheet, raise the jib, crank the winches, became increasingly difficult as his paralytic symptoms began at age 39 and worsened year after year. Most days his walking capabilities were poor to nonexistent; other days were even worse.

When he had his most severe neurological episodes, it was the National Naval Medical Center, the Bethesda Naval Hospital where he was taken, cordoned off on his own private floor, with his own doting private physicians. But it was the young, bright, caring doctor, the one who sat by his bedside and listened, who drew his admiration and respect, time after time. He was dignified, warm, and insightful.

"Son, you have been at the top of your class at Harvard Medical School. You have won the highest awards granted by the American Academy of Neurology. Dr. Israel Lavovsky, I ask that you be my personal physician," said the Commander-in-Chief. "My job is physically and emotionally draining. Ten, twelve, fourteen, sometimes twenty-four-hour days. These are trying times. You need to keep me healthy. I need help controlling these legs, my upper body, my mobility as best as is humanly possible. I need you to help me perform my presidential duties optimally."

"I'd be honored, sir."

***

Izzy was appointed Neurological Specialist and Head Physician to this brave but secretive man…secretive about his health, his politics, his prejudices, his loyalties, his decision-making, and his love life. The young physician, at the top of his game, forthright, patriotic, new and scared, stared down the hall at the door behind which, leg braces and all, sat the man who literally carried the weight of the entire globe on his shoulders.

Chapter 36
The Superfluous Ones

November 10, 1938, 6 am: Still in his bathrobe and pajamas, FDR's chief of staff reported on the latest of the German Reich's atrocities. The president, along with the rest of the world, was rocked by Kristallnacht. Hitler's National Socialist Party henchmen had attacked and destroyed synagogues and Jewish homes, schools, and businesses throughout Germany, killing over one hundred Jews and dragging 30,000 Jews off to concentration camps.

***

Among hundreds of items of correspondence, FDR received an avalanche of letters from Rabbi Stephen Wise, who organized various Jewish organizations and movements throughout the United States. The worsening crisis of the Jews in Europe became impossible to ignore. Just days before Roosevelt's 1937 inaugural address, Rabbi Wise, in a letter to FDR, informed him that at a recent session of the Polish Parliament, the Minister of Foreign Affairs, declared "that of the three and a half million Jews in Poland, three million are superfluous...."

Fear oozed through every crack in American society. In the face of the Great Depression, at least half the country stoked isolationist rhetoric, as well as racial prejudice and fear of foreigners taking jobs away from ordinary citizens. Pressured by the likes of the German American Bund, and the Christian Right, FDR also felt the squeeze from several of his Jewish advisors such as Samuel Rosenman, Felix Frankfurter, and Secretary of the Treasury Henry Morgenthau Jr. FDR failed to persuade Congress to pass less restrictive immigration laws in order to increase the quotas for German/Austrian and other European Jewish immigrants. The antisemitic isolationist factions in the country referred to his policies as the "Jew Deal."

Simply put, when it came to the European Jewish crisis, FDR continued to find his hands shackled. The president received hundreds of letters a week. Many praises. A flood of threats. But what about that strange, menacing letter his secretary showed him a month ago? A warning about the German Jews from some wise-guy in the underworld claiming to be the head of the American Crime Syndicate? Surely, something needed to be done. What or who would force his hand? He was unaware that the pressure would come from an unsuspecting source. An incredulous *quid pro quo.*

Chapter 37
Life and Death in Cuba

"Boychik, I need you to take a little trip to Havana," said Mr. L. to Nikolai as they were having coffee in the Boss's "office", the back booth in his favorite Jewish deli on Collins Avenue in Miami.

"You'll go to see a very good friend of mine, General Batista, the new president of Cuba. Bring your wife. She'll have fun."

"Sure thing, boss. Thanks. She'll like that."

"He's asked me to organize and reform the legal gambling institutions in his country. We've planned this over seven years. He and I have dreamed of creating the Monte Carlo of the Caribbean. All high class. The best of everything. All above board. And he wants us to begin with the Hotel Nacional. But that will only be the beginning. I'll go over the designs with you, the numbers, the personnel estimates, the projected overhead and profits. Of course, Batista will get his share. He's a general now."

Two years of bliss. The Steins had a beautiful apartment in Hollywood, north of Miami. Nikolai drove a Master 85 Chevy. Because of Mr. L.'s influence on the East Coast and around the country, Miriam had the privilege of hiring the best talent the country had to offer for his top-of-the-line casinos and nightclubs. No strangers to his clubs were Billie Holiday, Mildred Bailey, Sarah Vaughn, Frank Sinatra, Bing Crosby and, of course, the "Queen of Jazz," Ella Fitzgerald. Mr. L.'s clubs included The Colonial Inn and The Boheme in Hallandale Beach, Florida. Similarly, Moishie's entertainment account appeared to have no limits as he booked the likes of Benny Goodman, Duke Ellington, Count Basie, Tommy Dorsey in the summer in Saratoga Springs, New York and in Fort Lauderdale/Broward County, Florida in the winter.

As one might expect, Nikolai moved up in the ranks, to where he was essentially the impresario of not only Mr. L.'s hotels and casinos in Florida, but the many Saratoga lake´ houses ...The Arrowhead Inn, Piping Rock Club, The Chicago Club, The Mayfair, Riley's Lake House, to name a few. Nick traveled back and forth, winter and summer, from

Florida to Upstate New York and back again. But he loved it. Everyone in the organization trusted him.

Nothing but the best food in the restaurants. Nothing but the classiest entertainment in the nightclubs. To be clear, save for Las Vegas, gambling was illegal in the US. To be even clearer, Nikolai knew. Moishie knew. Miriam knew. These enterprises amassed huge profits. The "skim" was bigger than huge.

Over the last many months and years, while the Steins worked diligently for Mr. L., making his casinos the most elegant gambling meccas in the country, they could not possibly be immune, could not possibly ignore the comings and goings of the most notorious gangsters in the country. Men like Bugsy Siegel, Lucky Luciano, Longy Zwillman, Joe Adonis, and Frank Costello. Payoffs to cops, politicians, city or county or state officials did not go unnoticed. Mr. L. and his people were given a chance, a choice, and knowingly took it. And why not?

Perhaps there is a biological or inbred tendency to take the other path, the one that promises something for nothing, the road where the risk is high, the reward is high, but at the cost of practicing illegal, immoral behavior where others on the bottom rung inevitably get hurt. Is it one's inherent instincts, one's DNA that coerces them to choose the dark and winding road?

***

"Hurry up, Miriam. We're going to miss our flight to Havana. Mr. L. has arranged a private plane for us. And the car he sent around for us is waiting."

"OK. OK. I'm coming. Hold your horses. I had to pack things so I would look nice in front of El Presidente."

"And watch out for those mail jockeys," warned Mr. L.

"Those what, sir?" asked Nikolai.

"Those guys who fly the planes back and forth. Most of them are drug runners. They're cowboy-fliers. Keep an eye out. It can be a little sketchy down there sometimes."

***

The presidential palace military escort picked up Miriam and Nikolai at the Havana Airport. While they were being sent to help establish a gambling empire, they did not fully realize the economic situation in Cuba. If the Great Depression had brought the US to her knees, it had completely devastated Cuba. The economy was in shambles. During the 1930's, Cuba was plagued by continued worker strikes, industry shutdowns, military juntas and coups, student protests, closing of schools and universities, pro-government and anti-government demonstrations. Some of the short-lived government regimes were brutal.

Over the last few years, Fulgencio Batista was the de facto leader of Cuba, the man who pulled the strings. He promised to rebuild the economy, upgrade schools and universities, kick-start businesses, and invest in the sugarcane and tobacco workers. Best of all, he promised to bring tourism back to his beautiful island by supporting and reforming legal gambling casinos, seaside hotels, and nightclubs. He wanted no drugs, no heroin, no smuggling. The chaos in the streets would be quelled by his military.

"It's a dreamland," Mr. L. had said. "Casino gambling is completely legal there. And the Cuban government has asked me to organize gambling reform. Best of all, we will be supported and welcomed with open arms by my very good friend and partner, el Presidente."

***

The couple sat with General Batista for two days, several hours a day, reviewing plans: costs, personnel, architecture, interior design, financial arrangements, recruitment of talent, and, of course, profits that Mr. L. projected for Hotel Nacional Casino. They planned a Moorish/Seville style façade and Art Deco interior. It was majestically perched on a cliff overlooking the aqua waters of Havana Bay where the Gulf of Mexico meets the Atlantic. They talked of other soon-to-be-built hotels and casinos, (especially the planned Hotel Riviera, which in years to come would be the sparkle in Mr. L.'s eyes). It would not be completed for another two decades.

El Presidente wined and dined them. He regaled them with his humble beginnings in the sugarcane fields of the province of Holguin. Having joined the military, at the age of thirty-three he helped lead the anti-government "Sergeants Revolt," establishing him as the puppet master of Cuban politics. He improved public works, expanded the educational system, fostered growth in the economy, while expanding his connections to the underworld. Plots were brewing. He warned of danger in the streets. As a military power broker, he told them of his need to recently put down several oppositional forces. At the completion of their discussions, the two bagmen for Mr. L. deposited two large suitcases of currency for Batista.

***

"Hey, Nicky, let's not waste these last two nights. Let's go to some clubs. Live a little. Have some fun. This is a chance of a lifetime. We can check out the entertainment scene for Mr. L."

"Anything you say, baby."

They hit the streets. For two nights they sang and danced and listened to music. The Cuban rum was sweet intoxication. As they stumbled out of the Tropicana II on their last night, a stranger grabbed Nikolai's left arm and pulled urgently.

"What the hell," Nick said, struggling to shake loose. On her right, a man grabbed Miriam from behind and shoved them both toward a black car, engine throttling, double parked on the street.

"Hey, who are you? What are you doing?" cried Miriam, kicking and punching the stranger.

At just that moment, out from the shadows, eight Cuban military officers appeared with night sticks. Four grabbed the two assailants, and dragged them a way. The car screeched away.

"Babe, are you OK?" asked Nicky.

"Yeah, I guess so," Miriam said in a shaky voice.

"Wow. Where did you come from?" asked Nick, turning toward the remaining policemen.

"We've been here all along, senor," replied the officer.

"Wait, you were following us the whole time?"

"Of course, senor. Did you think the president would want you off by yourself, unprotected in Havana? Now let's get back to your hotel. I am sorry that our Welcome Wagon has been not so welcoming."

***

"Well, at least we're both OK," said Miriam, back in their hotel room preparing for bed. She walked across the room and gave Nicky a hug. She shifted her thoughts to music.

"I don't know, Nicky. There's something about this Cuban music we've heard. The brass, the maracas, and the clackers. A rhythm, a beat, improvisation, with flavors of African, Spanish, Indian, South and Central America. The sweat. The fast pace."

"To me, our jazz has this energy, this rhythm, this soul. It makes you want to feel. This Caribbean music makes you want to come alive."

"I know what you mean. It's a vibe we can corral from here and transport to New York and Miami. Oh, by the way, honey, let's take the boat back over to Miami tomorrow."

"No, Nicky, the seaplane was so great. We can take a boat any old time. Besides, I heard there's a storm between here and Key West."

"OK, whatever you say."

***

As they drove at dusk through the poor, crowded streets of Havana on their way to the airport, a monsoon erupted. When they reached the airport, they ran from the car onto the drenching, windy tarmac and onto the waiting plane. As they ran up the wobbly stairs to the plane, they heard, "Hurry, Senor and Senorita. Get on board quickly. We want to beat this storm."

As the plane lifted off, the first roll of thunder sounded and the sharp crack of lightning lit up the right side of the craft. Nikolai peered out the window of the four-seater craft. The rain was blinding. Visibility became non-existent. The crackling of thunder was ear-splitting and lightning illuminated the sky like thousands of camera flashbulbs. Nikolai felt like an ant inside a can being kicked down the road. The plane tilted from side to side, lifting and heaving, until his stomach was in his throat.

"Don't worry," said Nick. "We'll be OK." He squeezed Miriam's hand.

"We have to be," said Miriam, "We promised Moishie we'd be home for opening night."

"We'll be OK. According to my watch, we must be over the Keys. We only have a few more miles to go 'til we touch down in Miami."

Miriam's heart was hammering. The wind blew mightily from all directions. The plane was sinking. Images of her life, her family, her children raced through her mind. They saw no lights below.

***

Mr. L.'s driver waited on the tarmac in Miami for over two hours. No touch-downs. No arrivals from Havana. Just rain and wind that uprooted palm trees and knocked down telephone lines. The driver finally drove back from the airport to report to the Boss.

Chapter 38
Surprise

The first meeting was bleak. Very bleak. Words didn't come easy. Shocked. Stunned. Devastated. Tears welled. Just when the world seemed right-side up again. Just when he and his parents were getting to know each other again…stories to be told, truths or half-truths to be related. No warning. No fairness. No right or wrongness.

As for Mr. L.'s attempt to empathize, to offer his condolences…well? He was used to dealing with gunshots, stabbings, slit throats, a strangulation perhaps…but a small airplane crash? And yet they talked. About their heritage. About the business. About life choices. Like father to son? Son to father? Grandfather to grandson? But talk was cheap. Losses were not. Like you are finally holding on to a trusting hand, tight, never to let go, and suddenly it let's go with a ripping force. You feel an ache like you've never felt before. Terrified, you look down at the hand, moving away with no arm or body attached. In its grasp, is your heart.

***

Moishie threw himself into his work. Over the next weeks and months, he talked often daily with his mentor, especially during the winter months when the Florida casinos and nightclubs were hopping. Mr. L. began sending Moishie more frequently up North to the Saratoga clubs. His fondness and trust in his handler had grown. Moishie loved running these beautiful casinos tucked away in the foothills of the Adirondacks. "August was the place to be" pronounced the Saratoga Race Track (the oldest in the nation). It was another of Mr. L.'s profit centers. It was exciting.

Moishie enjoyed the train ride to Upstate New York, especially the ride through the Hudson Valley along the Northern Hudson River with its wildlife of American Eagles, Canada geese, red-tailed hawks, and green-headed Mallards. The changing foliage from spring to summer and into autumn grew on him…a home-coming of sorts, back up North. It was the summer of 1941.

"You're doing a great job, boychik. The casinos and nightclubs, both north and south, are making a bundle. Don't worry. I got another crew handling the Cuban operation. I need you in Saratoga. Some changes are coming. War? No war? You know, boychik, we're already helping our country…this great country that has made us rich and is now being attacked by Nazi U-boats. The German American Bund has organized in every major city, spreading antisemitism, isolationism, and lies."

"I know this country means a lot to you. And the same goes for your Jewish heritage. You still want to be buried at the Mount of Olives Cemetery in Jerusalem near your grandfather?"

"Yes. If they'll have me. We came from Russia, Poland, Lithuania, all over. To Palestine, to America. But I am who I am. I am nothing if I'm not a patriot. A Jew who is willing to destroy every last fucking Nazi. Yeah, of course, we're a crime syndicate. Do you think the US Navy wants it known they asked us to protect our waterfronts in every major seaport… New York City, Newark, Philadelphia, Los Angeles? The government knew we controlled the docks. It was all hush-hush fulfilled our duty against those Nazi bastards slipping ashore on their U-boats. We saw to it that not one of those bastards would see the light of day if they tried to supply their subs at any major port."

"That was you? Your guys?"

"You bet your ass it was. And hell, what about those fucking German American Bund assholes and their summer camps? Kids marching, singing, parading in their brown uniforms to those swastika flags, all over the fuckin' country, especially on Long Island. Can you believe the US government asked us, Murder Inc., to fight those Nazi hooligans? They called on me, us, our guys, on the QT of course. And boy, did we crack some heads. People think us Jews are soft. We survived the pogroms, came here with *bupkis*, and made our way so we would never be kicked around again. Well, we showed them. And with our help, our protection against the enemy just miles off our coastline, do you think the feds owe us something? I do."

***

After another successful season in Saratoga Springs, Moishie was ready for the winter casino operations in Florida. But things had changed. FDR had declared war on the Empire of Japan and on Germany and Italy. With declaration of war, it was not clear how business was going to be. All the crews at all the casinos were preparing as usual, for the high-rollers, the rich snowbirds to flock down South for the expected glamour, entertainment, and high stakes. For only the second time, Mr. L. asked Moishie to come to his home, "for a little talk."

"Listen, Moishie. You and I are like two peas in a pod. Family from the old country…making our way in this new world. You're young, early thirties, smart strong, but alone. You've lost most of your people. I have a crippled son, another daughter and son who don't talk to me, a first wife who is in and out of institutions, and a second wife—don't get me started. Us? We are family. You and I. This is our family. "He spread his arms out to the many framed pictures of his cronies scattered around the room.

"You're my only family now."

"And who are we? We're gangsters. We're patriotic Americans. We're Jews. Tough Jews. Well, our people are getting their asses kicked in Europe. Rounding up hundreds of thousands of our people, shooting them, forcing them into labor camps where God only knows what happens to them. And that president of ours is doing nothing."

"What can we do, Mr. L.? Clearly you and your guys have tried to beat those bastards," said Moishe. "I even know that you have personally given a lot of dough to that woman Goldie Meyerson from the Jewish Agency/Labor Zionist Party to help the Jews in Palestine."

"Yeah, she goes by Golda Meir now. But there's something I want to talk to you about. One reason I brought you down here…you and your family, God rest their souls. I thought Nikolai would be carrying out this plan, but it has now fallen on you."

"What? What plan, Mr. L.?"

"A plan to help our people. A plan that I will discuss with you. A plan I need you to carry out in the near future."

"Me? What can I do? I manage casinos and play the trumpet."

Mr. L. exhaled the smoke from the last drag on his cigarette, stuffed it out in the big glass ashtray, and looked up at Moishie.

"This will involve both you and your brother," said Mr. L. quietly, head down, raising only his pupils and eyebrows toward Moishie.

"But sir, with all due respect, I don't have a brother. I had a sister once, but she died of polio when we were kids. She was eight years old. I was ten or eleven. That was over 20 years ago."

"Yes, you do, Moishie."

"Mr. L., I don't mean to be rude, but I do not have a brother."

"Moishie, with all my contacts, all my investigators, all my snitches, all my government, journalistic, and political stool-pigeons, have you ever known me to be wrong about my, shall we say, reconnaissance?"

"But I swear, Mr. L. Of course, I would know if I have a brother...."

"Moishie. Calm down. Just calm down. We'll talk about this. And about the plan I have for you. I trust you. I will be counting on you."

Chapter 39
Autumn, 1942: First Part of the Journey

A plan of plans...well thought out, at least at first blush. Mr. L. always planned meticulously. He paid attention to every detail. A prodigious plan. Thorough down to the last item. What could go wrong? Maybe everything.

The train ride was different this time. Moishie, season after season, had taken the train up from Florida, spring blossoming in Upstate New York in May, emerging from the depths of a cold winter. The Hudson and its estuaries would glide along, no longer icy or snow covered, as the train rambled along, swaying back and forth. The leaves of the maples and white beech seemed to open just as he'd reach each station along the picturesque landscapes of painters like Thomas Cole and Frederic Erwin Church. The fragrance of the lilacs and hyacinths reminded the region of a redolent Spring.

The scenery this time looked more like his autumnal ride *back* to Florida when the temperature dropped, the leaves were all aglow. On this ride, the birds were flying south and he was travelling north *from* Florida.

It was an elaborate plan. One that only Mr. L. could have hatched. Details, perhaps too many, had been worked out. There was a deep-seated passion in this assignment. Bold. Risky. And full of surprises.

"So about your brother. Moishie, if you think long and hard...you may remember a time, several months...you would have been, oh, maybe five or six years old. After your sister died. Your father had visited you and left again, back to Detroit. Seven months later, your mother left the house and left you in the care of your Grandma Lewinski," said Mr. L. softly.

What was he saying? Craziness—at first. But slowly, a vision, of his father gone again...his mother now gone...his sister gone and now alone in the house. No one.

"Your mother. She couldn't handle it. Absent father. She felt she had no choice. She went to one of those homes for wayward mothers. She had a healthy baby boy."

"Wait, wait, wait, Mr. L. Are you trying to tell me that I have a brother somewhere?"

"The baby was a Jew baby. Nobody wanted a Jewish baby. There was only one agency in Boston to place Jewish babies into Jewish homes."

"And so, you're telling me I have a brother hanging out somewhere that I haven't known about 'till now? And how do you know all this?"

"Don't you know I got my own investigative reporters? For the last time, there is little I can't find out through my sources. I got as many inside people as our friend Hoover. But this brother of yours isn't just hanging out somewhere. Let me tell you about him."

As the cold rain pelted the train window, a thick fog obscured the western shore of the Hudson River. The train sped north on the eastern shore from Yonkers, to Croton-on-the-Hudson to Peekskill, to Beacon, to Wappingers Falls, and on up to Poughkeepsie.

What had he been told? The truth? Was it part of Mr. L.'s attempt to coax Moishie into this scheme? His entire family gone and now…?

As dusk approached, the train stopped at the Poughkeepsie station. Moishie picked up his suitcase, walked onto Platform A, down the stairs and then up the stairs to the opposite side of the tracks to Platform B. He stepped onto train number 4, going west over the river as he'd been directed to do. Train number 4 was an extension of the Maybrook Railroad line of New York, New Haven, and Hartford Railroad. The Trans-Hudson Bridge was a double track railroad bridge completed in 1889. In a few minutes the train rolled over to the western shore and stopped in Highland.

Moishie stepped off the train, walked through the station exit, and waited on the curb. It was dark and misty and the rain had stopped. Within a minute, a black Chevy Cabriolet pulled up alongside Moishie. From the half-open passenger window, a driver in a grey fedora, white shirt, black tie asked, "Stein?"

"Yes."

"Get in."

Moishie looked straight ahead into the darkness as they drove west in silence and then took a sharp turn to the south. Up and down a rolling country road until the sign said, Newburgh. So far, so good. No glitches. The easy part.

***

"So next, you'll be driven to the home of a friend of mine, Don Petrelli. Good friend of Dutch Schultz. You know, AKA Arthur Simon Flegenheim. Another yid. Tough guy. Crazy, if you ask me. Dutch used that place as a safe house when things got too precarious, if you know what I mean," said Mr. L.

"You'll stay there overnight. Couple of days. My guy Dom will provide you with a car, and a partner. You then hightail it to this Tuxedo Park joint."

Again, an easy part. The next part? Not so much.

***

How could Moishie have said no? Mr. L. had provided for his family, for him. He trusted and supported him like a grandson. Helped him hone his managerial skills, his confidence. And now he had no choice. He didn't want a choice. He had come to honor and respect this *alta kocker.* He would complete this assignment for the only family he had left.

"So you mean, this younger brother of mine that you claim I have, are you telling me he has lived all these years just ten miles away from me on the other side of town? With his ordinary family in South Boston?" Moishe shrugged, hands in his pockets.

"Oh, he's no ordinary kid."

Moishie stopped. He lowered his head. And almost in a whisper, said softly, "Tell me the truth. Did my father Nikolai know?"

"You know, Moishie, I'm not sure."

Mr. L. took a long drag on his cigarette, the fourth in the last hour. Smoke poured out of his nose. He snubbed it out.

"Not ordinary, you say? So what's he like? 'Moishe stood and closed his eyes, rubbing his temples between his thumb and other fingers.

"Well, like you, he is musically talented like your father and your grandmother before you. Violin. Smart like you too. Graduated Harvard College and Harvard Medical School. Skipped a few years even. Navy paid the whole deal."

"And so he's a local doctor somewhere around Boston?"

"Well, not exactly, Moishie."

Mr. L. lit up another cigarette and took a long, hard drag, as if hoping to help him find the words.

"What do you mean? He's not a doctor anymore? He became a lawyer? He died? What? What?" With a sweaty brow, Moishie prompted his boss for the straight answers.

"Well, to tell you the truth, your brother, Dr. Israel Lavovsky, Lieutenant Commander in the Navy, is now the personal physician to the President of the United States of America."

Moishie's eyes widened. The skin of his temples tightened. His senses shutting down. His jaw dropped and his mouth flew open, but no sound came out.

Chapter 40
Meet Sam

Dominic Petrelli's two-story Spanish-style home on the corner of North Street and Carpenter Avenue in Newburgh, New York, featured a large white marble gurgling fountain in the front. A bucolic pinewood forest fanned out in the back, covering five acres. The house was no ordinary one. It was a safe house for Dutch Schultz and his cronies in the past, as Moishie learned when they led him to a padlocked door in the basement on day two. Don directed Moishie to follow the middle underground tunnel that traversed below the wooded area for three hundred yards, leading to a set of concrete stairs. At the top of the stairs, a trapdoor opened onto the forest floor. He inhaled the fresh scent of the white and red pines. He was told he would be met by a black Ford Deluxe Club Coupe on the lonely road just beyond the opening. Sam Levine would drive. He was head of the Jewish hit squad for Mr. L and Lucky Luciano.

The car pulled up on the north/south road skirting the property as soon as Moishie emerged from the woods. Sam was in the driver's seat. A huge guy, red heaped-up scar across his lower forehead almost closing his left eye, and a ragged pink line running from behind his right ear down to his jugular. He was a survivor. They drove to Tuxedo Park in silence. The rain had stopped, the sun was shining, the temperature had now risen to the high sixties. The skies were clear, the air was crisp, as the Ford pulled up to the Blue Ribbon Diner off Main Street. The two men entered the diner, sat down at a booth, and talked about their next move over a cup of coffee.

"What are two Feds like you doing up here in this quiet neck of the woods?" said the waitress with a wry smile as she poured coffee. The two guys wore tan trench coats, fedoras, white shirts and black ties, plain grey trousers, and scuffed black no-name shoes.

"Making sure it stays quiet, honey," said Sam.

"Now look," said Mr. L. "My man, Sam, has already made a dry run. You'll proceed up a hill, and at the top you'll be introduced to the world of the truly rich and famous. Mansion after mansion like you've never seen. Backyards as big as Yankee

Stadium. Tall brick or stone walls that got everything but the barbed wire shouting 'keep out, you don't belong here.' But the Tower House. You can't miss the place. It's got this five-story castle-like tower on one side. Tallest mansion in the whole neighborhood. Belongs to a weird guy named Loomis. He turned the place into some kind of science laboratory. Invited the biggest brains in the world. Loomis puts them up. Mashugana. He's crazy. But he's filthy rich. Gardens, tennis courts, a pond. It's like one of those freakin' monasteries. I got a guy on the inside who will unlock the back gate. Huge wrought-iron thing. We know our target's schedule. You just grab him and take off. Piece of cake. Sam will take care of the rest until you get to Hyde Park. You got all this, boychik?"

They left the diner and drove up a winding road to the top of a hill overlooking Tuxedo Lake. They saw walled estates protected by tall hedges, allowing one an infrequent glimpse into the properties. Imposing gates obscured long driveways leading to mansions of granite, marble, and brick. Many had expansive wrap-around porches and gazebos off in the distance.

"Holy shit," said Moishie. "I've never seen anything like this."

Having done his reconnaissance, Sam slowed the car in front of an enormous edifice, Tudor in style, made of both Yonkers granite and Onondaga limestone. The five-story tower loomed large on the left side of the gigantic stone structure crowned by a crenellated wall circumnavigating the top of the tower. The car almost stopped in front of the polished black and gold iron gate. The latter was wedged in between two imposing gray granite pillars marking the beginning of a crushed stone driveway leading to the Tower House. The car rolled slowly past the entrance and circled around the opposite side of the property. In the back, in the shadow of a great oak, Sam killed the motor. The two men sat in the car, silent, waiting for the precise time to make their next move. Moishie squeezed the passenger door handle.

"Sit tight," grunted Sam. "Our target will be here shortly."

Chapter 41
Enclave of Excellence

Just north of Tuxedo Lake, heading toward the Catskill Mountains of Upstate New York sat Tuxedo Park, a town of 600. It was not difficult to imagine that the elegant gentleman's formal dresswear had it's origin in this posh, resort-like neighborhood. Sam had driven along the rural mountainous road in order to skirt the local road from Newcastle to Haverstraw. A left turn westward along the west bank of the Hudson brought them through Pomona, Montebello, and Suffern. A sharp northward turn, up rural Route 17 brought them through Sloatsburg, and finally around the northern bend of Tuxedo Lake. Who knew? Why Tuxedo Park? And who was this Alfred Loomis character anyway, the proprietor of the Tower House, the target property?

***

Alfred Lee Loomis was a private man, eccentric, born to blue blood East Coast heritage, bright, inclining toward the edge of brilliance, who seemed always to carry an aura of secrecy about him. Yale, Harvard, Wall Street investment banker, he cashed out before the 1929 Crash, leaving him with a mountain of cash. Having escaped the destructive forces of the Great Depression, this eccentric tycoon, philanthropist, and society figure quietly receded, oddly enough into a world of scientific luminaries. There he used his enormous wealth and determination to surround himself with the brightest scientists and leading physicists of his day. Despite the path that his life had taken him through the pre-WWII era, he had housed a lifelong penchant for scientific research, theory, and invention, particularly in the realm of physics. Visiting Berlin in 1938, he was appalled at the advanced state of German scientific research and weaponry development.

Loomis returned to the US determined to devote himself and his resources to recruiting the most lauded scientists and engineers in the nation. He was intent on developing a world-class laboratory in order to expand the knowledge of the universe as well as to defeat the Third

Reich's military-industrial complex. He purchased the Tower House in Tuxedo Park, Orange County, New York, and established the Loomis Laboratory, 40 miles northwest of New York City.

Tuxedo Park was an ultra-exclusive community, an enclave of palatial mansions owned by tycoons, international cooperate executives…in short, a neighborhood of the filthy rich, snuggled in the Ramapo Mountains, a chain in the hills of the Appalachians.

The financer built a private complex of scientific laboratories and provided his visiting scientists with stipends, living quarters, and state of the art equipment. The property included tennis courts, extensive gardens, bridle paths, a nine-hole golf course, horse stables, and a small arboretum. In short, this philanthropist provided a dream-come-true atmosphere to study in peace, unimpaired. Albert Einstein called it "a palace of science."

Loomis appointed the eminent experimental physicist from Johns Hopkins University, Robert J. Wood, as the director of the labs. Together they recruited world renown physicists including Niels Bohr, Leo Szilard, Enrico Fermi, Einstein and other preeminent scientists of the day.

The secret Tuxedo Park labs produced several world-changing discoveries, including exact measurements of time, precise muzzle velocities of wartime artillery, and global long-range navigational systems (the prequel to GPS navigation). It was the ground-breaking experiments with ultrasound radiation that would eventually lead to the invention and implementation of RADAR. Eventually, the US government demanded control of this project, having experienced abject failure in defending against German U-boats off the American coast. The federal administration convinced Loomis and his scientists to move the entire ultrasound radiation project to M.I.T. This colossal effort became known as the RAD LAB. With continued financial and organizational support from Loomis, Allied scientists established the concepts, developmental design, and production of RADAR (Radio Detection And Ranging) system. They produced RADAR before the Germans, encouraging many to say that "it was RADAR that won the war, the atomic bomb that ended it."

But the two thugs sitting in the black sedan at the rear of the property that autumn day were interested in only one of the brilliant scientists working within the walls of this enclave of excellence…a young genius who had recently emigrated from Italy

***

Einstein learned of his past German colleagues' discovery of nuclear fission in the summer of 1939. The first nuclear reaction was designed and built by Robert Dobel in Leipzig, Germany in June 1942, but an explosion ensued. The reactor never got up and running again. Germany never pursued a nuclear program thereafter.

Loomis, a staunch patriot, began to shift the laboratory's investigations almost solely toward wartime technologies. Einstein and Leo Szilard wrote to FDR in August of 1939, informing the president of Germany's potential nuclear threat and its implications. This provided a major spark that ignited the start of the Manhattan Project. In December 1942, Dr. Enrico Fermi built Chicago Pile-1, the first self-sustaining nuclear chain reactor, one of the most important components of atomic bomb production.

***

Dr. Enrico Fermi, world-renowned physicist, took his regularly scheduled afternoon walk past the gate in the rear of the Loomis property. He had just arrived two weeks ago as a visiting professor. He noticed a change in the cool autumn air. He heard the soft breeze blowing the red and gold leaves from the giant maples. He was pondering the new group of his brilliant colleagues the president of the US had recently called together to build a weapon of mass destruction, an atomic bomb. He was asked to be one of the leaders.

He did not hear the opening and closing of car doors just outside the security gate. Neither did he notice the locked wrought-iron gate swing open just behind him as he strolled, deep in thought. He had used electrons, and protons, and neutrinos as targets in many experiments over the years. Never did he imagine that he too, might be a target of a different sort.

Chapter 42
The Target

As Professor Enrico Fermi meandered along the path beside the lily pond, he was not thinking of pions, or neutrons, or chain reactions, or mathematical formulas. He was worried about his wife Laura and his two children, twelve-year-old Nella and seven-year-old Giulio. They remained in the flat in Manhattan while he took this short sabbatical to the Loomis laboratory to join his physicist colleagues Neils Bohr, Leo Szilard, and Edward Teller. He watched the German American Bund parade down Fifth Avenue a few weeks ago. He and his family left Italy for the USA to escape the antisemitic forces that were peaking in his native country. His wife and children were Jewish. Had they jumped from the frying pan to the fire?

His head ached. Looking down at the ground as he walked, he didn't notice the two men approaching him.

"Excuse me," said the taller one with a scar over his left eye. "Are you Dr. Enrico Fermi?"

"Yes, yes, I am. And who are you?" The scientist slowed. His neck muscles tensed.

"We're federal agents," said the smaller, handsome one. "We're sorry, but you have to come with us. Now." Dr. Fermi looked into their menacing faces. No smiles. Blank stares.

"What's this about? I've done nothing wrong. How did you get in here? Is this about the work I am doing? Is my family safe?"

"You'll find out when we get to headquarters," said Moishie as he stood directly in front of the target. Sam slipped around behind Dr. Fermi, placed his hands on either side of his neck and squeezed. The world-renowned scientist stopped talking, his eyes rolled back, and he slumped over.

"Quick, put his arm around your shoulder," said Sam.

With an agent on either side, they dragged their victim off the path, threw open the gate, and shoved him in the back seat of the car. Grabbing some rope from the trunk, Sam tied hands and feet.

"Get in. We gotta go," he growled at Moishie.

***

Fermi awoke in the back seat of the sedan. He looked around, felt the tightness in his ankles and wrists, and said, "Who are you? Where are you taking me? What do you want?" Silence.

"What's this all about? And why am I tied?"

Silence.

"Please. I didn't do anything wrong? Are you German agents?"

Silence.

Then, "Calm down, *dottore.* With your Italian accent, I can hardly understand you. We're government agents. We're going for a little ride. No one's going to hurt you. We're taking you to see someone very special," said the huge, scary bald one.

"You'll be alright," said Moishe.

"What about my family? Please don't hurt my family."

"No one wants to hurt your family. Don't worry."

"Why are you doing this?"

"You're needed for a very special assignment. You'll be safe. You'll be back doing your experiments in a few days. You'll be told more soon. Now, again, sit back and if you know what's good for you, you'll be quiet for the rest of the ride."

The car motored through the rolling hills of Upstate New York.

German agents? thought Dr. Fermi. *What was happening to him now? And when? Who would notice that he was gone? What will happen to his wife and children? Where were these thugs taking him? How could he get away? He was a scientist, not Houdini.*

He was thirty-eight years old. A year ago, he won the Nobel Prize in Physics. Columbia University hired him where he and his team performed the first nuclear physics experiments in the United States. He was recruited by the University of Chicago in order to build the first ever working nuclear reactor.

Surely, they will kidnap me, bring me to Berlin, and force me to reveal my scientific knowledge. The race is on. Who will build the first atomic bomb? Had he left his homeland Italy with his family two years ago to escape Mussolini's antisemitic edicts, only to be whisked away to the power-hungry claws of the Nazis?

They crossed the Hudson River and headed north. Enrico read the roadside signs: Beacon, Wappingers Falls, Crown Heights, Poughkeepsie, Hyde Park. Silence.

They slowed down.

"Hey, where are you taking me? What do you want with me? Are you German? Are you Russian?"

"All in good time, doctor. Pull in here," said the younger, kinder one.

They pulled into the driveway, toward the red, white, and blue sign: Presidential Motel.

"Hey, what is this? Where are we?"

***

He sat on one of the twin beds in the musty room, staring at the peeling, yellow paint around the doorway.

"What is this place? Why have you taken me here?" sighed Dr. Fermi, head down, raking his jet-black hair.

"Because we want you to meet someone very important. Someone very famous."

"Here? Here? In this filthy place?"

"Don't worry. Where we're going from here is nice and clean. Right up the road."

"Who is this famous person we're going to see? Some gangster friend of yours?"

"Not quite," said Moishie. "If you really want to know, I'm taking you to see Franklin Delano Roosevelt, the President of the United States of America."

Chapter 43
Impending Doom

Lieutenant First Class Israel Lavovsky played Stravinsky's violin concerto in D in his room at The Big House, down the hall from the thirty-second President of the United States. He was placed there purposely so that, as FDR's personal physician, he could attend to him at a moment's notice. He was thirty-one years old and had his whole life ahead of him. This assignment was the pearl of all assignments. But the schedule was grueling. Wherever and whenever the president moved, he would follow. Be that land or sea or air. At a minute's notice. Back and forth from Washington, DC to Hyde Park, down to Warm Springs, Georgia for the therapeutic baths, to secret rendezvous with heads of state in Malta and more. He was alerted by Secret Service that FDR had a secret meeting in Iceland in two days. They'd be flying there and returning by ship. Izzie had to prepare for anything and everything.

I can't imagine a more stressful job, thought Dr. Lavovsky. *How could the strain not affect the president's health? FDR had several hospitalizations in the past months. Entering the war, at the provocation of Pearl Harbor and at the ferocious pleading of Churchill, completely reversed the country's insistence on isolation for any number of political, economic, cultural, and religious reasons. They'd grown close,* thought the doctor, *and he cherished sharing thoughts and concerns with this clever and determined leader.*

Izzie and his boss had discussions on multiple occasions regarding the extermination of "his people" at the hands of Adolf Hitler. Atrocities and genocides were being perpetrated in the Pacific Theater by the Japanese. Communism spewed forth like the primal eruption of a volcano, its hot lava oozing over the four corners of the earth. The man down the hall balanced the world on his shoulders. Izzie couldn't let anything happen to him.

Israel had little family—adopted mother and father. No siblings. He felt part of the family at the Roosevelt home, Springwood. And he was treated as such. But the tension at Hyde Park, in Washington, in the country as a whole was at an all-time high. With the Depression, a deep divide in the country on many fronts, and declaration of war, Izzie saw trouble ahead, more trouble than the country and world had ever seen. A feeling of impending personal unrest was niggling at him as well. And he wasn't ready for any of it.

Chapter 44
Dealing with the Final Solution

FDR sat at his desk, a replica of George Washington's, stewing over the worsening crisis of the Jews in Europe. The two large windows straddling the painting of the *USS Dyer* on the wall behind him gave a clear view of the cool, crisp autumn day outside. He ruminated on the days just before his second inaugural address. Sources revealed to him that the Polish government had declared three million Jews "superfluous." He purposely included in that address, words to the effect that no law-abiding citizen of the United States would ever be considered superfluous.

The Jews constituted 3.69 percent of the US population. A large fraction of the Gentiles were clamoring to continue the restriction of Jewish refugees into the country from Nazi-occupied Europe. People were afraid. The public needed a scapegoat to blame for the Depression...someone to blame for taking the scarce jobs that were available. Though he and his wife Eleanor tried, no one wanted to lift the restrictive quotas of Jewish immigrants, including Congress. Even before declaring war, in his fireside chat of September 3,1939, he tried in vain to appeal to the nation's moral sense, meanwhile walking the tightrope of the wave of isolationism: "This nation will remain a neutral nation, but I cannot ask that every American remain neutral in thought as well...Even a neutral cannot be asked to close his mind or his conscience."

Not only was the most popular figure in America, Charles Lindbergh, railing against the Jews and for isolationism, but one of the most successful corporate leaders in the US if not the world, Henry Ford, was spending millions to sabotage rights of Jews at home and abroad.

And the letters. They poured in, hundreds a week. Many praising his policies, but he received an equal number of condemnations. Outright threats. Crazy. Like that one letter he received a few months ago from some Mafia figure. That one bothered him. Deeply personal. Promising to harm him, his family, and the nation. He gave it to Hoover at the FBI.

The Germans were secretly pouring money into Nazi propaganda in America. Goebbels' propaganda machine was pressing Americans toward isolation, "America for Americans." German-leaning journalists, authors, and community leaders convinced Americans that the Jews were responsible for the world's problems. FDR felt otherwise. He felt cornered. What was he to do? Who or what was going to force his hand, provide him with the answers? He did not know, but had a gut feeling that something was coming soon that would do just that.

Chapter 45
My Brother's Keeper

Moishie and Sam drove Professor Enrico Fermi from the motel down to the end of River Street in Hyde Park where a Baby Garwood roundabout was tied to the dock on the Hudson. Fermi's hands were still tied and his mouth now taped. They climbed aboard the boat and motored north. They soon reached an elaborate dock and boat launch. The dock was surrounded by sturdy stainless-steel handrails. On one side was a hydraulic lift designed to transport a person onto a waiting craft. A long, wide metal walkway was folded and leaned against a connected boathouse.

"No guards, no Secret Service detail?" Moishie asked Sam.

"We took care of that. Dogs too." replied Sam as he motioned his captive out of the boat and toward the shore.

"And take this. Just in case you need it." Sam shoved a snub nose .38 into Moishie's coat pocket.

"But I don't…" They all stepped up the ramp to the wooded shoreline. The trail up the embankment was paved. Halfway up as the terrain leveled, railroad tracks appeared and continued through the woods, north/south, until they bent into the forest. Close to the trail, stood a locomotive and one attached passenger car in tow.

"Direct shot to New York City and DC for the Old Man," whispered Sam. Still no one in sight.

Just ahead through the grove of fir trees was the rear of The Big House, FDR's Hyde Park mansion and expansive gardens. Still no guards, no police, no Secret Service. Not even a single guard dog. Sam continued to push Fermi forward until they reached a rear entrance. Moishie turned and stared at Sam for a moment with half-closed lids, his scalp tight, forcing his ears back. As Moishie entered the house, Sam whispered, "We'll stay out here. When I get the signal from you, we'll come in."

Moishie crept down the dark hallway guided by the soft violin music that was strangely relaxing. Dark mahogany paneling. Worn oriental carpeting. Lighting low. Noticing the next door slightly ajar, Moishie squeezed in and shut the door behind him.

Navy First Lieutenant Israel Lavovsky looked up and stared. His violin clattered to the floor. His gaze froze on the man standing in the doorway.

Like a mirror, he thought. His eyes locked on this doppelganger...the nose, the eyes, the lips, the chin. How could this be?

Getting up from his chair, Izzie backed up a few paces, unable to turn his head away. *Where's my revolver*? he thought.

"Hey, who are you? What's going on? How'd you get in here?"

"And you forgot 'why does it seem like I'm looking in a mirror'?" said Moishie. He couldn't keep his eyes off his brother.

"Yeah...right," said Israel backing away.

"Well, Izzy, why don't you stop worrying where your firearm is at the moment and let's talk about the answers to some of those questions." They both were trembling.

"What the hell is this? How do you know my name?" growled Izzie, throwing a glance toward the shelf where he stowed his unused military-issued pistol.

"Your weapon has been, let's say, *confiscated*, and I happen to have a .38 snub pointed in your direction at the moment. Now, sit down. Let's talk."

Chapter 46
What Will You Do?

Three knocks on the window. Sam pushed the physicist through the rear door, down the long hallway, and into Lavovsky's quarters.

"Well, ain't this a sight for sore eyes. A picture of brotherly love. Now let's get on with it," said Sam with a cold stare. Israel stood. Shoving him back down in his chair, Sam snarled, "Not you, Doc. You and I are going to stay right here, nice and cozy."

"You're going to need this," said Sam, handing Moishie a Bowie knife with an eight-inch blade.

"Now get going."

Chin on his chest, Moishie turned to his brother Izzy and said, "This is just something I need to do. Just following orders. Just so you know, there is no Secret Service on duty. There is a sharpshooter with a high-powered rifle trained on FDR right now. At my signal he will assassinate the president if you or Doctor Fermi do not follow orders. You and I will talk again later. Let's go, Professor." Doctor Lavovsky sat rigid in his chair, face flushed, glassy-eyed as his brother disappeared after shoving his captive through the door

Moishie pushed his abductee down the hall until they reached the door at the end. Suddenly, he pushed his prisoner through the doorway and stood behind him, knife to his neck, pulling hard on the ropes binding his hands.

"Hey. What is the meaning of this?" cried the president. "Who the hell are you? How in God's name did you get in here?" Bespectacled, gritting his teeth around his ivory cigarette holder, FDR sat frozen in his wheelchair at his desk, his brow glistening with sweat. He pushed hard on the button inside the first drawer without releasing his finger. His face was scrunched. His bushy eyebrows nearly touching.

"Never mind me, Mr. President. I am not here to hurt you. I'm only the messenger. But you will recognize Dr. Enrico Fermi, the preeminent physicist, perhaps second only to Einstein himself. Nobel laureate in 1938, leader of the F division of your esteemed Manhattan Project. The genius who developed and built the first nuclear reactor in this country.

The man who, if he lives, will be responsible for winning the race to the bomb."

"What bomb? What in holy hell are you talking about? Who filled you with this nonsense, this cockamamie information? Untie this man. I am calling my security."

"Mr. President, there are trained marksmen with their sights on the two windows behind you. Strangely, there are no Secret Service, no cops, no FBI, no guards anywhere in sight. Your phone wires have been cut. The alarm buzzer on your desk has been inactivated. But let's forget about all that."

With the sharp knife blade held firmly to Fermi's neck, Moishie said, "FYI, this message comes from a very powerful man whose identity will remain unknown."

"What in damnation is this all about? What do you want? Have you lost your damn mind? I'll have you shot on sight. Imprisoned for life if you survive."

"I suggest you listen, sir, and if I were you, I wouldn't move that wheelchair one inch. Let's talk about moral issues, why don't we? What about antisemitism? Don't you care about humankind? Hitler came to power in 1933. You have done virtually nothing to protect the European Jews. He has marched into Austria and Poland, and walked into Czechoslovakia like a hot knife through butter. Still nothing. You have kowtowed to the isolationists. You have allowed the growing number of fascists in this country to control you. Just what have you done for the Jews as they are being slaughtered by the thousands, hundreds of thousands, some say, millions?"

"Who are you to question my morals? My actions? What was I to do?"

"You could have joined England and France sooner. You could have had planted spies documenting the locations of the death camps the Nazis built throughout Europe. Special agents to interfere with the Nazi war machine, their transportation system, their stinking cattle cars carrying tens of thousands of innocent people to certain death. You could have helped the Jews fleeing Europe…expanded the immigration quotas.

"Who the hell are you? God knows we have tried. What the hell do you know? Let this man go and leave these premises immediately."

"Does the name the *St. Louis* mean anything to you? Hundreds of Jews got sent back from your shores only to be sent to their deaths in German camps. You could have granted a safe harbor, an asylum to the Jews for whom the death knell has been ringing throughout Europe for a decade now."

"I don't know who you think you are, young man. Do you think I didn't want to increase the quotas for Jewish refugees coming into this country? You think I didn't want our boys to join the freedom fighters in Europe? We have declared war. Our men and women will now fight this tyranny, this threat to world security, freedom, and peace."

"Words, words, words. Your fireside chats mean nothing if you don't stop this Nazi maniac. I'm sure you know the value of this man standing in front of me at knifepoint. You have recruited the brightest scientists in the country for the Manhattan Project. You have given them a charge, one of life and death, in a race to reach the potential of nuclear activity. And that race will be severely hampered, to say the least, if Professor Enrico Fermi is not a leader in that effort. I am standing here, risking my life, asking you to promise that you will do everything you can to stop the killing of my people, the people of your own personal physician, the people of this man's wife and children, the people of Einstein himself."

"How in heaven's name do you have access to our top secrets? Bewildering. What do you and your hoodlum cronies know? Can you see into the minds of the likes of Stalin? This monster Hitler has amassed a powerhouse of military might the likes of which the world has never seen. Right under our noses. I am afraid I have allowed myself to fall prey to the enormous political pressure that this devil and his following have forced upon my country and the world," said FDR, shifting in his wheelchair. "Do you have any idea of the monstrous influence that this Father Charles Coughlin has over the voters? His stronghold over congressmen, church-leaders, community leaders, spreading antisemitic lies throughout every corner of this country?"

"We must beat the Germans from harnessing and releasing the forces, both good and evil, that nuclear reactivity holds," said the president. "It is true that this remarkable man before me holds the key to defeating that systemic ethnic cleansing machine. I give you my word, going forward, that I will do everything in my power, by George, to put an end to the extermination of your people. For God's sake, release this man. You may be right about one thing. He may well be our last hope."

"But who do you think you are?" shouted Moishie.

"The Great Oz? Hiding behind the curtain, behind the skirt of your wife Eleanor, only to find you have no courage, no heart, and now I can see, no brain either? And it's the voters, you say? Not the American citizens, not the Jews in Europe, not the human beings being slaughtered. Yes, the very person who cares for you, literally keeps you from falling, keeps you out of the hospital, sticks to you like glue wherever you go, and services your every medical need…is a Jew. And you, *el Presidente*, refuse to use your power, your heart, your soul to save these Jews from certain death."

Moishie suddenly twisted the rope binding Fermi's hands, and pushed the knife-blade more firmly against his neck.

"If you know what's good for you, Mr. President, you will keep your promise to try harder."

Moishie, leaving the sweaty-faced world leader hunched over his desk, turned around, pushed his captive out through the doorway, and rushed for Israel's room.

Chapter 47
The Getaway

Once inside his brother's room, Moishie fixated on Sam's face, a smirk from ear to ear. Sam's gun with its silencer hung by his side. Moishie gazed down at the floor where Israel lay sprawled out in a pool of blood. Moishie's face drained. His heart stopped. His eyes bulged. His knees gave way, but somehow, he grabbed onto his captive and remained standing. His nostrils flared. He glared at Sam.

"Why, you dirty bastard." Moishie lunged at Sam, knife in hand. He stopped short as the murderer pointed his gun to his forehead.

"Expendable," Sam shrugged.

"You fucking monster," Moishie screamed, tears rolling down his face.

"The Doc was expendable. But we gotta move now before the whole world comes crashing down on us." Moishie stood paralyzed, glaring at the murderer.

Sam grabbed Professor Fermi, pushed him down the hall and out the back door. Fermi tried to scream. Only muffled sounds. Moishie, silent, instinctively ran down the hall, down the path, down the embankment, through the woods, over the railroad tracks, barely knowing how he got to the dock.

"Hurry up. Get in. We gotta go," said the scar-faced man standing at the wheel, having just untied the bow rope. Fermi sat on one of the boat seat in the rear. Moishie stepped into the boat and stood behind Sam.

BANG! Sam collapsed. A huge bloody hole in the back of his head. Moishie let out a blood-curdling scream. He pushed the thug overboard and jettisoned the murder weapon. With Moishie behind the wheel, the sleek Harwood motorboat roared down the Hudson River. Tears poured down Moishie's fire-red face. They didn't cool his pain.

***

The afternoon sunlight reflected off the shiny hull of the hardwood craft as it sped downriver. Neither man spoke. Moishie drove the boat, stiff, wide eyed, ignoring his passenger. The hawks and bald eagles glided high above, and the forest trees on either shore were bursting with brilliant colors. As the boat careened close to the western shore, Dr. Fermi, mouth taped and hands tied, stood up and swung his right leg over the front seat. Wobbly, with a wide gait, he moved slowly toward the frantic boat driver. The boat suddenly swerved to the right. The world-famous physicist stumbled, fell back, and flew headlong into the starboard gunnel. Moishie slowed the speedboat toward the isolated dock shrouded by a grove of overhanging sugar maples. Holding the boat steady against the dock, engine still running, he growled, "Get up and get out." Dr. Fermi struggled out of the boat and onto the dock.

"Stand over there," he indicated a spot on the dock 15 feet away. Moishie placed the knife on the dock, dug a set of keys out of his pocket, and placed them near the knife.

"Car's at the end of the path. Go save the world." And with that, Moishie gunned the throttle and roared off. He didn't bother to wave.

***

He finally had time to think. Moishie felt safe and sound for the first time in months. Only dark shadows filtered through the windows as the night train rumbled east. He had just returned from the dining car. Double bourbon. Neat. He couldn't escape the images…his brother, ghost white, blood soaked, sprawled on the floor… fleeing from Hyde Park…dropping off Dr. Fermi at the dock…anxiously motoring down the river and tying the boat at the far end of the Poughkeepsie Municipal Marina? He had to race to the train station and leap onto the train just leaving the station for Boston.

What the hell was he doing?

What had he done?

Where was he going?

Boston?

And when he got there, who did he know? Nobody.

Chapter 48
Duty Calls

It will only be a matter of time thought Moishie, as he roamed the downtown streets of Boston. He'd been looking over his shoulder for days. Strangely, several weeks ago, the Uncle Sam recruiting sign appeared like an oasis to him. He recalled his father's tales. He now stood in line, duffle bag over his shoulder, waiting for the bus to take the recruits to their pre-deployment training base.

"Hey, how ya' doin'," said the big, tall, muscle-bound recruit behind him. "Aram Moravian here. What's your name?"

"Moses Stein. Hey, you look like you can pack a punch when you want to. Ever been in the ring?"

"Once or twice."

"Maybe you'll think about heavyweight when we get to Fort Jackson? You might need a manager."

"Maybe. Hey, what about you? Why did you sign up?"

As Moishie stepped onto the bus, he looked back at Aram and said, "Oh, me? My brother just asked me to stay out of trouble."

Chapter 49
Family

He sat in his usual booth, at his usual deli. His white Pekingese, Benny, sat quietly next to him. The borsht was good today. Hot.

"Mr. L., one of your guys brought over a letter for you," said the waitress. Mr. L. put down his spoon and wiped his mouth. He picked up the envelope and opened it.

Mr. L.,

My brother Israel, my only family, got his. You'll get yours.

Moishie

Read on for a sneak peek at Goodman's next novel in

The Odessa Trilogy

THE NOBLE PHYSICIAN

Chapter 1

The Resurrection

All was quiet on Lake Talooska. As the sun began to fade, a slight chill pervaded the air at the end of that first day of autumn. He walked back to the cabin carrying the fishing rods, tackle boxes, and a string of tiny sunfish that his grandson David refused to throw back. A slight pinkish haze was beginning to form above the tall pines that surrounded the small New Hampshire crystal clear body of water. He walked up the short, well-worn path through the woods to their cabin, smelling the garlic from the chicken marsala that Marge had begun cooking for dinner. His favorite. Butch, their border collie, came out to meet him as he neared the end of the path, sniffed the fish briefly then quickly turned away with a sneeze of disinterest, happy to lead the way back to the house. The screen door slammed shut behind Becky as she walked inside with Speckles the cat in her arms, talking a blue streak about events only she and the cat understood.

He always felt calm, healthy, at the family's little slice of vacation paradise, except for the slight pain in his left chest, made worse as the weather began to turn cold. He had only vague memories of that fall day, almost a decade ago to the day. He was left for dead, lying in a pool of blood, at the home of the President of the United States in Hyde Park. Yet, Lieutenant Israel Lavovsky M.D., a neurologist and the personal physician of the President, somehow survived.

CHAPTER 2

THE INSTITUTE

After supper, he sat at his desk in his tiny office staring at the pictures on the wall. The sound of Rebecca's violin curled through the house, Brahm 's Violin Concerto in D. Yes, she had inherited the musical talent. The family elixir, no, the glue that bound generations of the family together somehow, stitched odds and ends of experiences, swatches of souls and events, bound together to form a garment that he hoped would surround and protect his loved ones.

The office was 10 by 10 feet. No windows. It seemed to some to be an add-on to the original cabin in the woods. The cedar wood clapboards on the outside had even worn a bit differently than the rest of the structure.

The pictures of his family competed for space on his desk...David in his waders holding up a fish bigger than himself, Becky stretching tall in her snowsuit next to a giant moose, Marge standing with her right arm making a muscle and an axe raised in the other, flashing that big bright beautiful smile in front of a pile of chopped wood, and of course, John.

The walls were covered with portraits …FDR, Truman, Admiral Chester A. Nimitz, Itzhak Perlman, Vladimir Horowitz, Dr. Jonas Salk, Dr. Albert Sabin, Dr. Milton Decker, Judea Pearl, Stuart Russell, Sigmund Freud, and other personal favorites.

He looked up at the picture of the fleet of battleships in Narragansett Bay, remembering the day, with a trembling hand…he picked up the letter on his desk for the third time and re-read it… "From the Admiralty's Office of the Department of the United States Navy…and because of the latter knowledge, expertise, and exemplary service you have rendered to your country, you are hereby appointed to be the first Director and Chief of Medicine at the Newport National Neurological Research Complex. This newly constructed $5,000,000,000 structure has been built in Newport, Rhode Island, on the property of the former

Newport US Naval Base, adjacent to the US Naval Academy Officers Candidate School. It is ordered that you present yourself at 0800 hours, 21 SEP 2010, at said facility. Further orders will be forthcoming…"

CHAPTER 3

THE RESEARCH

There had been thousands of labs around the world working to establish various cerebral networks, identifying newer neurotransmitters, establishing previously unknown neurological circuits, microwaves, gamma waves, newly derived biochemical substances, numerous microbial agents, and the list goes on. Trying to learn about 1 billionth of the brain's hidden capacity had eluded the most brilliant scientific and medical minds of the time.

But, what if the problem was turned on its head? What if one could BUILD A BRAIN, an intelligent organ/machine? A being…that could eventually itself learn how to figure out the workings of the brain? ARTIFICIAL INTELLIGENCE.

Thomas Goodman
The Odessa Trilogy

I

II

III

ABOUT THE AUTHOR

Following a rewarding career as an oncologist/hematologist, Thomas Goodman published his first novel in *The Odessa Trilogy*, The Bookie's Daughter, in 2024. It's the heroic story of a young woman physician/scientist who discovers the cure for cancer. The Road from Odessa, his second novel in the trilogy, tells the stories of young Moishie Stein, his father, and grandfather, a Jewish Russian mafia boss. They struggle amid family loyalties within the interweaving worlds of jazz and racketeering in Boston, Detroit, Miami, and Upstate New York. Dr. Goodman lives with his wife, Cynthia, in Upstate New York.

PHOTO CREDIT

The back-cover image is that of the Odessa, Ukraine seaport circa 1900-1914. From Picryl, "The world's Largest Public Domain Media Search. Permission for the use, reuse, or additional use of the image is not required. The image is a public domain photograph of a historic park (Odessa Harbor view), 19th century vintage card, free to use, no copyright restrictions image"-according to Picryl.

www.ingramcontent.com/pod-product-compliance
Lightning Source LLC
LaVergne TN
LVHW090513110826
845146LV00003B/839
9798994877227